THE MIGHTY

AMULET BOOKS · NEW YORK

AMY IGNATOW

ABRAMS The Art of Books
115 West 18th Street, New York, NY 10011
abramsbooks.com

To Anya and Ezra,
my very favorite Oddities

The Muell

Four Students Taken to Muellersville Memorial After Bus Crashes

A DISTRICT SCHOOL BUS returning to Muellersville from a daylong trip to Philadelphia skidded and overturned on Old Twin County Road last night, district officials said. Four middle school students and a trip chaperone were taken to the hospital with minor injuries, but the driver fled the scene and has yet to be found. Police are investigating.

THE DAILY WHUT?

Here's a weird news item—a bus flips over, a bunch of kids are taken to the hospital, and the driver . . . disappears? In the middle of nowhere? How is that possible? Was he picked up, and if so, WAS THE WHOLE THING PLANNED? Certainly someone would have noticed a soaking-wet, possibly injured man running away from the scene of the crime. And yes, I call it a crime, because vehicular manslaughter is a crime. Sure, the guy didn't kill anyone, so it's not technically manslaughter, but it could very well have been. So it's vehicular kidhurting. Any of my readers out there with a law degree want to weigh in on this one?

The problem with people today is that no one asks questions anymore, and we've all just become complacent sheep who think, "Oh, the bus crashed and the driver disappeared. Well, at least the kids"—KIDS!—"have only minor injuries, so it's all going to be okay." Well, sheeple, it's not going to be okay. Who's to say that Mystery Driver won't show up driving someone else's bus? YOUR bus?

Keep asking questions,
The Hammer

9

T WAS 6:30 A.M. AND THERE WERE TWO BUSES PARKED IN front of Deborah Read Middle School: a big, shiny Auxano Company coach with individual padded chairs, built-in television screens, and electrical outlets in every row, and—parked right in front of it—the Farm Kids minibus, which was short, yellow, and old, with duct tape–patched benches and windows that could only open three inches.

"We HAVE to get on the company bus," Jay Carpenter said to Nick Gross, "and we have to make sure that we're SITTING near the front so we can control the DVD player." His eyes were shining with anticipation. "I brought DVDs."

Nick was tired and cold, and it was too early in the morning to deal with his best friend's delusions. "Like they're going to let you play your DVDs. No one is going to want to watch a movie. They're all going to be doing test prep stuff." Nick was nervous about the upcoming statewide exam. It was a big one. Not that Jay cared. He had always been a "good tester," whatever that meant.

"O ye of little faith!" Jay exclaimed, entirely too loud for the hour and setting. Jay might have been better at academics but Nick was sure that he was smarter, because he'd never exclaimed "O ye of little faith!" in a high-pitched voice in front of . . . well . . . anyone, but certainly not in front of members of the opposite sex, who were milling around in their own pre–field trip cliques. Not that any of them would ever notice Nick.

But still, it was better not to start the day on a deficit by acting like a huge socially awkward nerd.

Nick watched as Paul Yoder and Sam Stoltzfus and the rest of the Farm Kids edged farther away from the little yellow bus that traveled forty minutes each way to take them to and from school every day. He couldn't blame them for not wanting to spend another four hours on it.

"It's not like I brought my DVDs of classic *Doctor Who* episodes!" Jay continued. "I know my audience."

"Fine, I'll bite. What did you bring?"

Jay opened his enormous backpack and began rooting through it. It was kind of hard to tell if he had the world's biggest backpack or if it just seemed big because Jay was so scrawny. It was sort of amazing that he could even lift the thing.

"What do you have in there?" Nick asked.

"Only necessities, my good man," Jay said. Nick shuddered inwardly. He'd always hated Jay's tendency to talk like he was a character in a movie where guys wore top hats and women wore corsets, but he'd given up trying to change Jay's speech patterns and had instead been trying, unsuccessfully, to get him to lower his volume instead. It was an uphill battle.

Jay pulled a DVD case out of his pack. *"Evil Dead Two!"* he exclaimed triumphantly.

"There's no way Ms. Zelle is going to let you watch *Evil Dead Two*," Nick said.

"Why ever not?" Jay was indignant. "It's a great movie and Ms. Zelle is a woman of singular taste and beauty."

Nick blushed. Thinking about the science teacher always made him blush. "I agree, but . . ."

"There is no but. It is a brilliantly subversive piece of cinema that was created to intentionally mock itself! It's both a sequel AND a remake. Who wouldn't love that?" Jay's voice was getting higher and louder.

"It's a horror movie from the 1980s. No one wants to watch that at seven in the morning. People are going to be either sleeping or studying."

"Studying, schmudying," Jay said. "Did you know that The Hammer believes that mandatory exams are actually a secret government plot to identify suitable subjects for biological technical enhancements at a young age?"

"I did not know that. Because it's crazy." Jay was always quoting his favorite local conspiracy theorist blogger.

"Don't worry, I think you're safe," Jay said, diving once more into his backpack.

Nick wrinkled his brow, slightly insulted. "Wait, are you saying the government wouldn't want to do experiments on me?"

Jay ignored him. "I have more DVDs! Everyone appreciates options, even those who may not yet have acquired a taste for the high art of camp horror."

Nick shook his head and looked at the line that had formed at the door of the Auxano bus. The Farm Kids were in front, and even though there was no love lost between them and the Company Kids, the Farm Kids were not to be messed with. They were tall and strong and traveled in an intimidating pack. Rumor had it that Paul Yoder could lift an entire bale of hay over his head without breaking a sweat. There was no way they *weren't* getting on the bigger bus. Nick knew that even if he and Jay could somehow push their way to the front of the line, they still wouldn't be getting on. Every middle school had an unwritten code, and it was pretty clear about who got to ride on the good bus and who had to ride with a rusty spring poking him in the butt.

COOKIE PARKER SCROLLED THROUGH HER PHONE AS they waited for the bus doors to open.

"Oh. My. God." Claire Jones said, looking point- edly at The Shrimp. He was looking through a backpack that seemed big enough to swallow him whole. "Please tell me he's not going to be on our bus."

Cookie rolled her eyes. "Like that's going to happen."

"You never know," Addison Gesualdo said. "I bet Yo-Yo Sub is going to make him sit next to us or something."

Cookie, Claire, and Addison had been trying for the past two weeks to find a good nickname for Mr. Friend, the substitute teacher who always seemed to be at school, but nothing stuck. Claire had suggested "Puke Pants," after the greenish corduroys that Mr. Friend seemed to wear every day (did he have just one pair of pants or were all of his pants exactly the same? MYSTERY! Especially if Claire was right and he was dating their science teacher, Ms. Zelle, who seemed put-together enough to be able to date a guy with more than one pair of pants), but it didn't seem to fit. Emma Lee had chimed in with "Sub-Sub" ("Even lower than a substitute teacher," she'd explained, earning a withering look from Cookie, because *come on*.) Then, a few minutes ago, Mr. Friend had whipped out a yo-yo to entertain the arriving kids before the bus doors opened. A YO-YO. He had to be kidding.

Still, Cookie wasn't convinced that "Yo-Yo Sub" had staying power. Finding good nicknames was tricky business—find the right name and you'd basically created a person. Cookie glanced at a tall dark-skinned boy who was standing by himself near the minibus. Take that guy. Terror Boy. He might have had a name at one point, but no one knew it, because people had been calling him "Terror Boy" for as long as anyone could remember. The same was true of her own name. It was actually Daniesha, but her family had started calling her "Cookie" when she was little because she had told them that she loved cookies (although, really, what little kid doesn't like cookies?). Cookie doubted that most people even knew her real name. But she figured that it could have been much worse—little Daniesha could have told everyone that she loved hamsters, or farts. When you thought about it, "Cookie" wasn't so bad.

"There's no way The Shrimp is getting on our bus." Cookie stifled a yawn and shivered. "We'll make sure of it." The thought of listening to The Shrimp's high-pitched voice going on and on about *Star Trek* or *Star Wars* or whatever for two hours was unacceptable, and she wasn't about to endure it when there was a perfectly good other bus for him and his loser friend to ride. Time to do something about it.

"What are you going to do?" Emma asked nervously. She was always around. Emma had been hanging out with Addison and Claire, Cookie's best friends, since they were all in diapers. She was annoying. And she was clearly terrified of Cookie.

"Get Izaak over here," Cookie told Addison, ignoring Emma, "and tell him to bring everyone else." Cookie could have easily done this herself, but she knew Addison liked to have an excuse to talk to Izaak. And Cookie was good at telling people what to do. Sure enough, Addison scampered off.

Claire waited until Addison was gone. "So, do you think we will be able to find that store from the Constitution Center?"

"What store?" Emma asked. Cookie gave her a look.

"I'm going to go help Addison," Emma said, backing off.

Cookie had lived in Muellersville for almost as long as she could remember, but she had spent the first five years of her life in Philadelphia. Muellersville was nice and all, but Philadelphia (or Philly, as her family liked to call it) was a city. Philly was big and exciting and had more than two streets and didn't smell like cow poop. Any horse-drawn buggies were fancy tourist horse-drawn buggies, not weird Amish teenagers out for a joyride. Philly was also full of brown people, some of whom were related to Cookie. Her aunt and cousins still lived in Philly, and Cookie knew where to get the best Philly cheesesteaks and the best gelato and even where the best jewelry store was, because her cousin Zakiya had taken her there when she'd visited Philly over winter break.

When school had started again, everyone had noticed her

new ring, and Claire had begged Cookie to tell her all about the store. The store was like a fantastic secret for only cool people to share: there was no sign out front, you had to ring a buzzer to get in, and if they let you in there was a staircase that brought you down into a room with high ceilings and no natural light and then you were surrounded by display after display of the most amazing and strange jewelry you'd ever seen. There was a mysterious man with a handlebar mustache behind the display cases who hardly spoke, and you were lucky if he even sold you anything. Claire had practically drooled when Cookie had told her about it. And when they'd heard about the field trip to the National Constitution Center in Philly, she'd kept talking about it until Cookie promised to take her.

Cookie didn't totally know how to get to the store, but she was pretty confident that she could find it. They hadn't told Addison or any of the others about the plan, because the teachers would definitely notice if more than two people went missing for a few hours.

"And is it close to where the bus will be dropping us off?" Claire squeaked. She really needed to calm down—her hyper-excitement was going to attract attention.

"Sure," Cookie said. She was mostly sure anyway.

Addison and Emma came back with Izaak in tow. "What's up?" Izaak asked. He was almost the tallest boy in the sixth grade. Cookie suspected that Terror Boy was actually taller, but he had a bad habit of stooping over, so it was hard to tell. The group of boys that followed Izaak wherever he went hovered behind him. Like Izaak, they were Company Kids (children whose parents worked at Auxano, the company just outside of town that employed more than half the adults in Muellersville), and it was as if they never knew whether Izaak was about to have a private conversation or one that they were all invited to join. They had a tendency to shuffle awkwardly in the background.

Cookie smiled her very nice smile. "I just wanted to make sure that we're all sitting together," she said.

"No problem." Izaak grinned and made his way to the company bus. The doors opened for him as if by magic, because Izaak was one of those guys who had special powers that ensured that everything in his life was smooth and easy. He shoved The Shrimp's huge backpack out of his way, spilling DVDs, comic books, and who even knew what else all over the sidewalk, onto the street, and behind the big bus wheels. The Shrimp started shrieking his objections, but Izaak ignored him and climbed onto the bus. Everyone else followed. Emma unsuccessfully hid her giggles behind her hands.

"I guess we're getting on the buses!" Yo-Yo Sub yelped.

ONCE UPON A TIME, FARSHAD RAJAVI REALLY liked American history. He'd come home from school, itching to tell his parents all about what he'd learned—the "discovery" of the West Indies by Christopher Columbus, the thirteen colonies, the Declaration of Independence, the Revolutionary War, and on and on and on—and Dr. and Dr. Rajavi would listen and ask ques-

tions, because they genuinely wanted to learn, too. It would make Farshad feel smart. As immigrants to the United States, his parents didn't know most of what he was telling them. His mother knew all about working in a lab with chemicals and formulas, and his father understood complex mathematical equations, but Farshad knew about the history of the United States of America, and he loved it.

Well, not anymore. Now when he came home from school and his parents asked him what he'd learned that day, he didn't have much to say. He was learning, of course, but thinking about his school day wasn't something that he wanted to do, particularly since that day in fourth grade when Izaak Marcus came up with the brilliant nickname "Terror Boy."

That day had started off just fine, like any other day. His teacher, Mrs. Lehrman, had been talking about the Middle East and had asked him to tell the class what Iran was like. Farshad had just been there for a family visit during winter break, so he talked a little bit about the food he'd had, and his aunts and uncles. The rest of the class didn't seem particularly interested, so after a little while he'd just stopped talking.

The badness happened later that day at gym. Everyone was playing volleyball, which Farshad was good at. He was tall, which was a big advantage in volleyball and would always get him picked first by the team leaders. But that day he was picked last, after Jay Carpenter, who was about the same size as Emma Lee (the tiniest girl in fourth grade). It was confusing, but Farshad had played anyway . . . until Izaak knocked him down as they were both jumping to spike the ball. "Stay down, Terror Boy," Izaak had hissed at Farshad as he lay stunned on the floor. "So much for all your training."

Training? Farshad had been so confused. He'd never been to volleyball camp or anything like that, so he didn't know what Izaak was talking about. But it wasn't long before he understood that, until his little talk about the family's vacation to Iran, none of his classmates had ever really noticed that his parents weren't American. A kid like Izaak Marcus should never have that sort of information. All he had to do was give Farshad a cold shoulder and call him "Terror Boy," and from that point on it was all over.

Friends stopped coming to Farshad's house. It wasn't like when he was little and kids *had* to come over, whether they wanted to or not, because their moms set up all the playdates. They were too old for that now. When his birthday came around, he just told his mother that parties were for little kids. Farshad's mother believed him, because she figured that maybe this was how things were done in the United States. Maybe parties were just for little kids. It was as good an explanation as any for why he'd stopped being invited to them as well.

For a while Farshad was sure that everyone would get bored of calling him "Terror Boy" and move on to torturing some other poor kid for no good reason. But the name stuck. When he was out of school sick for a week it was because he'd gone to a terrorist training camp, where he'd learned how to set up a suicide bomb. The same accusation was whispered just because he was in the science club, even though, duh, both of his parents were scientists. Of course he'd be interested in the subject. When he did well at school, classmates would grumble that it was only because the teachers were afraid of him. Anyone caught trying to be friendly to him was given the cold shoulder by the rest of the class. Farshad Rajavi was toxic.

He'd hoped things would change when he got to middle school, but it was as though everyone from his elementary school had hung out with everyone from the other elementary school in Muellersville over the summer. In the fall, Farshad was Terror Boy again.

Farshad had spent most of that summer with his cousins in New Jersey. They were in high school, and when he'd told them about the whole "Terror Boy" mess they'd offered to come to Pennsylvania to "show those racists the true meaning of terror." At the time, he'd declined—the last thing Farshad Rajavi needed was for his brown-skinned, black-haired cousins to come storming up to Izaak and his friends and provide them with evidence of all the horrible things they'd been saying about him.

But it was tempting. There were days when all Farshad

wanted to do was call Mohammed and Sam and have them come over to show everyone that he was a protected man. An important person. A respected guy. But mostly he just wanted to disappear.

Farshad took one look at the big, shiny Auxano bus, where Ms. Zelle and Mrs. Whitaker were going over their class lists, and quietly stepped onto the yellow minibus. It was just easier. He took out his test prep book and settled in for the long trip to Philadelphia.

JAY SPENT THE FIRST HALF OF THE TRIP TO PHILADEL-phia bleating his outrage to Mr. Friend, who began to look distinctly less friendly as the sun came up. "We were at THE FRONT of the line, and WE SHOULD have been on THE BIGGER BUS." It was always interesting to Nick to hear which words Jay would emphasize—he was never predictable. "THIS bus doesn't even have a DVD PLAYER. And I brought ALL THESE DVDS!!! And for what? And why do we even need this second bus if there's only going to be five people on it! This is a waste of hard-earned taxpayer dollars . . ."

Jay wouldn't be able to keep up his lamenting for long; he never did. It was a pattern Nick knew well—some injustice, real or imagined, would befall his best friend, and Jay would rage on about it for a while until he realized that nothing could be done to rectify the situation. Then he would deflate and act sulky for about ten minutes, and then remember something from a comic book or a movie or some sparkly part of his crazy Jay brain where aliens rode pirate-treasure-puking unicorns, and then everything would be bright and shiny again. It was exhausting. But Nick was used to it. They had been friends for a long, long time.

Sometimes Nick wondered what it would be like to not be friends with Jay, but it was kind of unfathomable. Sure, Jay could be annoying and exasperating, and half of the trouble he got into could probably be avoided if he'd ever learn to shut up, but that was Jay. Jay was the kid who would climb a tree and sneak into his best friend's room to keep Nick company when his dad was sick in the hospital. Jay was the kid who saved the little snack packs from his airplane trip to give to Nick because Nick had never been on a plane before and wanted to know if food that had been at thirty thousand feet tasted different. Jay was the friend who had engineered after-school science tutoring with Ms. Zelle for Nick because he knew Nick had a crush on her. It was incredibly embarrassing and uncomfortable, but still, Jay's heart was in the right place. So, as annoying as

Jay could be, Nick could never picture them not being friends. Friends like Jay Carpenter didn't come around every day.

Jay had stopped harassing Mr. Friend and plopped down next to Nick. "This is an INJUSTICE. These windows only open an inch? I CAN'T BREATHE." He was angry but fizzling out. So predictable.

"You can breathe," Nick said, "and this bus is fine. Why would you want to spend two hours with those jerks anyway?"

"Oh, Nick. Nick, Nick, Nick. The other bus isn't full of jerks, it's full of beautiful ladies." Lately, Jay had been getting more and more interested in the female members of their class, which seemed deeply unwise to Nick. "If we had been on the other bus, we could have shown the ladies *Evil Dead Two*, and then the ladies would have been so scared that they would have jumped into our laps, because we are big, strong, protective men. Ladies like that."

"Say 'ladies' one more time."

Jay giggled. "Ladies. Layyyyyyydeeeeeeeez."

Nick laughed. "Well, they probably wouldn't have let us watch the movie anyway. I'm sure that Cookie Parker or someone brought some stupid chick flick to watch."

"Oh, shut down your tongue. Speak not ill of my darling Daniesha. She is a particularly fine lady."

"Cookie Parker would squish you like a bug if you got anywhere near her."

"To be squished by Daniesha Parker would be divine. Mark my words, Nick, my old and doubtful friend, one day she shall be mine."

"Really?"

"Yes, Doubty McDoubtpants. One day, my gorgeous Nubian queen will come to understand the glories of being with me, and we shall fall in love and make coffee-colored babies."

"Oh my god, please shut up."

Jay sighed. "Can you shut up love, Nick? Can you really?"

"I will give you a dollar to shut up." If Nick actually gave Jay a dollar every time he offered him one to shut up, he'd be in debt up to his eyeballs. But Nick knew that it was safe to make the offer, because there was no way Jay would ever actually stop talking.

DEEP DOWN, COOKIE JUST *KNEW* THAT LEAVING THE field trip was a terrible idea. First of all, Claire was quite possibly the world's worst accomplice. Her inability to keep calm made Cookie suspect that she might have had a latte or something equally caffeinated that morning, which meant that, in addition to being crazy jittery, Claire was going to start complaining about needing to use the bathroom, probably as soon as they slipped away. Another problem that Cookie wasn't totally willing to admit to herself was that she might not be completely sure about where they were going. She figured she'd kind of sort of recognize things as they got closer to the store. She remembered that it was on a tree-lined block and that there were a lot of cute boutique stores around. And maybe a pizza place across the street? How many places like that could there be in Philly?

"They're looking at us, oh god, they're totally looking at us," Claire whispered as they made their way to the front entrance of the museum. Unless they had secret eyes in their ears, Ms. Zelle and Yo-Yo Sub were definitely not looking at Cookie and Claire. The friends had spent a solid half hour in the museum with everyone else, waiting until the trip chaperones were nicely distracted by the exhibits. It was the perfect time to leave, as long as you weren't leaving with a shaking, twitching, sweating Claire Jones. She might as well have been wearing a

neon sign over her head that flashed LOOK AT US, WE'RE UP TO NO GOOD!! Cookie tried not to grind her teeth.

"Did you see what Bella Yoder was wearing today?" Cookie quietly asked Claire.

"Oh. My. God. YES. What is she, Amish?" Claire launched into a fashion critique. Cookie couldn't help but smile to herself. So predictable. Claire could probably face down a firing squad without so much as a bead of sweat if she was able to complain about the inherent awfulness of the Farm Kids while doing it. And that's how they got out without anyone noticing. Well, Emma Lee was watching them, but that didn't count.

✷ ✶ ✷

FINDING THE JEWELRY STORE WAS ANOTHER STORY, THOUGH.

"Seriously, where is this place, I need to pee," Claire whined. They had been walking down tree-lined blocks for what seemed like forever.

"Well, you can't pee in a jewelry store," Cookie growled, looking around for a chain restaurant where Claire could use the bathroom. "Here," she said, seeing a coffee shop and pushing an uncomfortable-looking Claire inside. "Go here."

The place was kind of dark and there were only a few people sitting at the tables, but they all seemed to turn and stare at the girls as they walked in. Cookie gave Claire a quick shove toward the back and then made her way to the counter, waiting until Claire was safely out of earshot. "Could I have some hot cocoa?" she asked the tattooed barista, whose hair looked like faded rainbow sherbet. Cookie hated coffee, but most of her friends claimed to love it, so she always tried to order something that looked like coffee in order to carry the cup around. And of course she had to order something, because this was the city and you couldn't just go into a coffee shop and pee in their toilet without buying anything. It's not like Cookie was some sort of ignorant country kid who didn't know the rules.

The cocoa was expensive. Cookie sighed and handed the money to Sherbet Head. This was the price of friendship—you had to risk your scholastic career just to drag your hyper friend around Philly and spend all your money on stupid overpriced cocoa so that she could go to the bathroom. Deep down in her heart, Cookie knew that she would probably have been happier just staying with the group and watching Addison flirt with Izaak, but she was Cookie Parker, of whom a certain level of awesomeness was expected.

PROBABLY HALF OF THE CLASS HAD SEEN COOKIE Parker and Claire Jones sneak off, yet somehow Mr. Friend, who was *right there*, had missed it entirely. Of course no one would say anything about it to him or Mrs. Whitaker. Farshad certainly wasn't going to. It was bad enough being called "Terror Boy." If he told on the girls, he knew he'd probably be called "Snitch Terror Boy" or something stupid like that.

The problem for Farshad, as far as he could see, was not that everyone hated him for no good reason. Okay, that was a problem, sure, a pretty big problem, but it wasn't the real problem. The real problem was that, if something were to happen to make people like him again, he would never be able to forget what rotten jerks they had been.

Farshad had been friends with Izaak once, sort of. If someone had asked Farshad a few years ago, "Are you friends with Izaak?" he probably would have said, "Sure," without having to think too hard about it. They'd been classmates forever, and were more often than not on the same after-school soccer team. Farshad's mother and Izaak's dad both worked for Auxano, so the boys would see each other at the company club and hang out at every company picnic, eating hot dogs and playing Frisbee with the other Company Kids. They used to have a good time. It was one of the advantages of being a Company Kid: Even if you didn't know everyone, Company Kids under-

stood one another and had each other's backs. Or so Farshad had thought.

For the past few years, Farshad had stopped going to the club altogether and worked to come up with new elaborate excuses for not going to the Auxano picnic. He fervently hoped each year that his mother would just stop asking if he wanted to go, but she persisted—the picnic was in a month, and already she was questioning his need to stay home to study for finals that wouldn't take place for another month after that. But his grades were exemplary, and even when his mom worried about why his friends never came over or why he was no longer interested in after-school sports, she couldn't deny that he was doing very well academically and was well on his way to becoming the class valedictorian. A completely loathed valedictorian, but she didn't know that.

The girls had been gone for a half hour and the teachers still didn't seem to notice that they were missing. Ridiculous. Maybe one day Farshad would stop being so surprised at how the adults at school kept failing him.

Farshad spotted Jay Carpenter standing among the bronze sculptures of the signers of the Constitution and was struck by a terrible idea. Before he could think too hard about it, he found himself sidling up next to the school's resident oddball. Farshad purposely dropped his test prep book on the floor.

"Hello there, butterfingers!" Jay said, bending down to scoop up the book. He was probably one of the few kids at school who was still clueless enough to talk to Farshad. He was also really loud. Conveniently loud.

Farshad took the book. "Thanks," he said, looking around the room. "Hey, have you seen Claire Jones? She wanted to tell me something," he added somewhat weakly.

"Wasn't she with Daniesha?" Jay asked his friend, and started scanning the room.

"Don't worry about it," Farshad muttered, and backed away. Jay Carpenter was like an incredibly predictable explosive and Farshad knew very well that he'd just lit the fuse.

WHERE IS DANIESHA?" JAY BLEATED. NICK HAD noticed her sneaking out with Claire Jones but hadn't mentioned it to Jay because—"Where is my beautiful black pearl?" Jay swiveled his head around Signers' Hall. He was being too loud again.

"She probably just went to the bathroom," Nick mumbled.

"No. No no no, impossible, because she went to the bath-

room right when we got here," Jay said, showing off his creepy awareness of when people went potty.

"Well, maybe she had to go again. She's a girl. Girls maybe can't hold it in as well as guys can."

"Nicholas. Now don't let me hear you making false and sexist statements. Daniesha Parker is a strong woman, and if she wants to hold it in, rest assured, she can hold it in." Jay began darting from statue to statue to see if Cookie was hiding behind any of them. He was making a scene. "Do you think we should tell Ms. Zelle or Mr. Friend?"

"No!" Nick blurted, and immediately felt embarrassed by his own volume. "No, no, we shouldn't . . ."

"Did I hear my name?" Mr. Friend sidled up to them. The guy was sneakier than your average yo-yo enthusiast (not that Nick actually knew any of those).

"No," Nick said.

"I haven't seen Daniesha Parker and I'm worried that something untoward might have befallen her," Jay explained.

"Jay, I'm sure Cookie is fine," Mr. Friend said, quickly scanning the room. Nick's heart sank. The hall was full of their classmates, and the fact that Jay just outright told one of the teachers that Cookie and Claire had left the Constitution Center was not going to go unnoticed. Or unpunished. Already he could see Emma Lee watching them, and Addison Gesualdo reaching for her phone to send a text that was probably telling

Cookie to get back immediately because Jay had blown their cover. Nick's mind raced desperately for a way to get out of the situation.

"I . . . I think they went to the bathroom," he said. Immediately Nick felt the heat rising up his neck to his cheeks. *Thanks, face, you pink jerk.*

"*They?*" Mr. Friend asked. "Cookie and who else?"

"I . . . I don't know." Nick had recently seen an article about sinkholes, which are a sort of natural phenomenon where the ground opens up and swallows everything within a large radius. He found himself desperately wishing that he had actually read the article instead of just looking at the photos so he could understand what exactly the chances were of one swallowing him up right at that moment. Mr. Friend excused himself and walked over to Ms. Zelle. "Oh god," Nick whispered to Jay, "she's going to check the bathroom."

"Good," Jay said loudly. "I for one will have a lot more fun on this field trip knowing that everyone is safe and accounted for."

Nick stared at Jay, and he wasn't the only one staring.

THE TEXT WAS IN ALL CAPS.

"We have to go," Cookie told Claire as she came out of the bathroom, showing her what Addison had written.

"Oh god. Oh god oh god oh god, what are we going to do???" Claire was squeaking and everyone was watching. Cookie grabbed her arm and steered her out of the café and back onto the sidewalk. "We are in so, so much trouble," Claire moaned. "So so so so so so so so much trouble!"

"Just shut up. Chill. Chill and shut up. We just have to go back to the Constitution Center, find the group, and pretend like we were there the entire time. If we act natural enough and really believe that what we're saying is the truth then everyone else will believe it as well." Cookie liked to think of herself as a generally good person, but sometimes even generally good people have to lie, and she knew that the best way to do it was to convince yourself that it wasn't really a lie. After all, they hadn't even made it to the jewelry store, so it was pretty much as if they hadn't left the field trip.

"They're looking for us right now! There's no way we're going to get back in time!!!"

Should I slap her? Cookie wondered. This calmed people down in movies. But Cookie had never actually slapped anyone before and, like with most things, thinking about it too much made her reconsider. *What if someone saw me do it? What if it made the situation worse?* She imagined Claire clutching her red right cheek, screaming and sobbing, and throwing herself into oncoming traffic. That would probably be worse.

Cookie looked down the street. "Okay, shut up, we'll get a cab."

"That's brilliant!" Claire looked anxiously hopeful. "There's one!" she squealed, waving her arms in the air. "Taxi!"

"That's just a yellow car," Cookie growled. The Slapping Option was looking sweeter and sweeter. She spotted a cab a block away. "There," Cookie said, pointing to it and taking a step back, "you hail that one."

The cab came to a halt in front of them and they scrambled in. It smelled weirdly of fake cherries. "Take us to the Constitution Center," Cookie said, trying to sound as authoritative as possible. "Please."

The taxi zipped through the city. Claire gripped her purse, her pale knuckles turning even whiter while Cookie went over the plan. "We're just going to tell them that we went to the bathroom and then got turned around, right?" Claire nodded silently as Cookie read Addison's text again. If they somehow managed to get through this, Cookie vowed to destroy that stupid Jay Carpenter. Actually, she was going to find a way to destroy Jay Carpenter even if they didn't get through this. *Especially* if they didn't get through this.

THE TEACHERS HAD FORMED A GROUP AND WERE talking worriedly among themselves. Clearly, if all of the bathrooms had not yet been checked, they would be soon. Nick could feel the storm of gossip starting to gain power.

"Dude," Izaak told his crew, "they are So. Screwed."

"So screwed!" Emma chimed in.

"I texted them," Addison hissed, eager to call attention to her heroic protection of the friends who hadn't thought to take her with them, "so they're on their way back."

Nick knew that he technically shouldn't be afraid of Cookie Parker. He was much bigger than her, and he didn't think she had any secret ninja skills. But still, Cookie could be . . . scary. She had a power that seemed to flow through her like the Force, only it wasn't a nice, peaceful, benevolent Jedi sort of thing, it was more of a *Cross me and I will destroy your face, puny mortal* sort of thing. She'd taken down kids before. Izaak might have been the one to start the whole "Terror Boy" thing about Farshad Rajavi, but it was Cookie who started the rumors that made the nickname seem less funny and more real. That kid went from being just a normal dude to being the most hated guy in school, and he hadn't really done anything wrong besides being better at volleyball than Izaak.

What would she do to Jay?

Then again, what could *she do to Jay?* Nick asked himself as he watched Jay take photos of the sculpture of Founding Father Richard Dobbs Spaight Sr. Jay was one of those rare, magical people who was able to float through life without any realization of or concern for what other people thought of him. Jay's complete cluelessness was one of the things Nick appreciated the most about him; it was also the first thing that he'd change, given the opportunity and a magic wand.

But what other kid would surprise his best friend by filling his room with balloons on his ninth birthday? Nick had spent the entire birthday in the hospital with his dad. His mom, aunt Jilly, and aunt Molly had tried to get him to celebrate, but it's hard to feel festive with your dad attached to a bunch of tubes with wires poking out of him. There had been so many blinking machines around his dad's hospital bed that it was hard to get close to him.

Nick's dad had wanted him to have a party at home, but Nick didn't feel good about doing it without him, so Aunt Molly had brought a small cake to the hospital. Some of the nurses had come into his father's room to join in singing "Happy Birthday" to Nick. His dad had put on a *Yay* face, but you could tell that everyone was thinking the same thing: This was probably the last birthday he'd be alive to celebrate. Nick had tried to eat some of the cake, but even though it was devil's food (his favorite), he had no appetite. After a few bites, he excused himself and hid in a hospital broom closet until his eyes were dry again. Nick was pretty sure one of the nurses knew that he was in there and kept guard at the door so he could be alone. His dad's nurses were always kind of great like that. Sometimes he missed them a little.

✳ ✳ ✳

THAT NIGHT, HIS MOM ORDERED PIZZA THAT THEY PICKED UP on their way home. They listened to the radio while eating dinner. She was tired; he didn't feel much like talking, and what was there to say? It's not like turning nine was that big a deal. Nick's mom had asked if he wanted to watch a movie or something and he'd said, "No thanks, I'll just go to bed," and then she did that thing where she hugged him a little too tightly. She stopped only when she realized that his air supply was being cutting off. Nick said good night and trudged up to his room.

When he opened the door, there was a split second where all he could see was this wall of bright colors, and then balloon after balloon came tumbling down on him. "Mom?" Nick yelled as the balloons bounced past him and down the stairs. "MOM?!?"

His mom was halfway up the stairs when she stopped, slack-jawed, to stare at the cascade of balloons tumbling out of Nick's room. "Oh my god," she said. "Jay was here when I came home to walk Shelly and asked if he could leave something in your room for your birthday."

"Did you notice that he was carrying a truckload of balloons?" Nick asked incredulously.

"No! He must have blown them all up himself!" His mom could not look away from the room full of balloons—they reached from floor to ceiling. "He must have been here for hours."

They stared at each other. Jay Carpenter had been coming over to Nick's house since he was old enough to pedal his tricycle, and it wasn't that unusual for Nick's distracted, upset mom to just leave him alone in the house. They looked back at the room and began to laugh. It looked like a giant gumball dispenser.

It took them about an hour to reach Nick's bed. Initially they tried wading through the balloons, but there were too many, so Nick's mom grabbed her long-neglected knitting needles and they went on a badass ninja balloon-stabbing spree. With every *POP!* they laughed harder. It was a ridiculous amount of balloons, a completely absurd amount of balloons, and popping them had been weirdly satisfying. Nick would never know if Jay had filled the room with balloons because he knew that popping all of them would be kind of therapeutic for Nick or if he'd filled the room with balloons because he was the goofiest kid alive, but it didn't really matter. What mattered was that Nick's best friend had spent hours pushing the air out of his narrow lungs to give Nick a happy birthday on one of the worst days of his life, and that was not something that Nick would ever forget.

Cookie was probably going to try to destroy Jay. But what could she really do to him? How could you destroy a kid like that? Everyone in the school already thought—rightfully—that Jay was a huge spaz. Jay was bulletproof.

But Nick wasn't.

THE REST OF THE FIELD TRIP WAS KIND OF A BLUR FOR Farshad. He went over his study materials, trying his best to concentrate on the information packet that Mr. Friend had given them and to take notes in the margins so he wouldn't be blindsided by the inevitable quiz on it back at school. But everyone kept buzzing about what had happened to Cookie and Claire. Farshad couldn't help but listen:

"I heard they got tattoos," Ramona Piña said to Makaela Jennings. "On their butts."

"Oh my god, what if Mr. Friend is making them sit down right now?"

"They totally got wasted," Izaak told his crew, who nodded in sage agreement, because two twelve-year-olds finding a bar in Philadelphia that would serve them at eleven A.M. was completely plausible. It was hard to believe that some of his classmates were the offspring of brilliant scientists. "Claire is so going to barf on the way home."

"Ewww!" Addison squealed, and Emma laughed.

Whatever theories the kids had, they all sounded cool, like Cookie and Claire had gone on a whirlwind tour of Awesomeness. Somehow, breaking the rules had solidified their popularity, which was ridiculously unfair. Farshad could disappear and return visibly drunk with the image of a beautiful woman's face covering his entire back and they would probably still think that he was out buying weapons of mass destruction. Not that he would ever get a tattoo of a beautiful woman's face covering his entire back, because maybe someday a girl would want to look at him without his shirt on and he didn't want her saying, "Uh, who's that?" But still.

At least Cookie and Claire would be getting in trouble—that was something. They *had* to be getting into trouble, right? The world was certainly not so cruel as to just let them off scot-free.

BUSTED. MRS. WHITAKER AND YO-YO SUB GRIMLY marched the girls to an administrative office, and Cookie could tell that Claire was having one of her silent freak-outs. It was a very bad sign; a chattering Claire was irritating, but a silent Claire meant that all of her anxiety and nervousness was building up inside of her and was sure to explode all over the place. It was like the time last summer when she'd had that crush on the teenage lifeguard at the Auxano pool. She, Addison, Emma, and Cookie had spent nearly every day at the club, and every time the lifeguard would even glance in their direction Claire would go catatonic with fear. This went on for a few weeks (and Cookie couldn't help but make fun of Claire's inability to speak), until finally one morning the lifeguard said, "Good morning" to the girls, and all the words that Claire had been stuffing into the back of her throat broke free and spilled out.

"HI HOW ARE YOU DO YOU LIKE BEING A LIFEGUARD YOU'RE SO BRAVE IT MUST BE SO HARD TO WATCH ALL THESE PEOPLE ALL THE TIME I COULD NEVER DO IT NOT THAT I DON'T KNOW HOW TO SWIM I TOTALLY KNOW HOW TO SWIM SO YOU DON'T HAVE TO WORRY ABOUT ME BUT THAT DOESN'T MEAN THAT YOU SHOULDN'T WATCH ME WHILE I SWIM JUST IN CASE I DROWN I'M JUST SAYING THAT I'M NOT A HIGH PRIORITY LIKE A FOUR-YEAR-OLD OR SOMETHING I'M DEFINITELY

OLDER AND MORE MATURE THAN A FOUR-YEAR-OLD AND SO HOW DID YOU BECOME INTERESTED IN THIS PARTICULAR LINE OF WORK YOU DON'T HAVE TO ANSWER IF YOU DON'T WANT TO BUT I'D REALLY LIKE TO KNOW BECAUSE YOU'RE REALLY INTERESTING . . ."

At first, Cookie and Addison could do nothing but help-lessly stand by. They had wanted to stop Claire, but it was like watching a train wreck in progress. Finally, Cookie had found her legs and did what any great friend would do—she hurled herself at Claire, sending both of them crashing into the pool.

Addison jumped in after them for good measure (or probably to avoid awkwardly standing with Hot Lifeguard), and Emma jumped in after her, because Emma always did what everyone else was doing. Claire had been super pissy at first, which was fair, because no one likes being surprise-shoved into a pool, but as usual she eventually came around to see that Cookie had been looking out for her best interests. She even thanked Cookie, as she should have—Cookie hadn't even been wearing her swim cap. Her mother had been furious with her when she saw the state of Cookie's hair. That was the last time she'd had it straightened during pool season.

Honestly, constantly looking out for everyone else was hard work.

Cookie knew that if Yo-Yo Sub and Mrs. Whitaker focused on Claire, she was going to break. Cookie had to go on the offensive.

"Are we in trouble?" Cookie asked in her most incredulous voice. You have to believe that you're truly innocent in order for others to believe that you're truly innocent.

"We're going to sit down and have a talk," Mrs. Whitaker said, opening a door to a windowless office with a table and a few chairs that was lit overhead by long fluorescent lightbulbs. Cookie wondered how many other kids had been brought to the Constitution Center Interrogation Room for questioning. Time for the outrage.

"Are we in trouble for getting lost?" she asked, getting a little louder.

Mrs. Whitaker and Yo-Yo Sub looked at each other, and for a moment Cookie could see their doubt. *Good, very good.*

"How, exactly, did you get lost?" Mrs. Whitaker asked, arching one eyebrow. Cookie had to admire the skill it took to arch just one eyebrow. Maybe Mrs. Whitaker's professors in Teaching College had seen it and suggested that she would be especially effective as a middle school teacher.

"I don't know. If I knew how we'd gotten lost then we would have been able to retrace our steps and find the rest of the group. Knowing where we were would have made us less lost." Cookie looked at them defiantly. It was possible that she and Claire could actually get out of this as long as Claire continued to keep her crazy mouth shut.

"Claire?" asked Yo-Yo Sub. "Did you know where you were?"

Claire shook her head. The crazy was building up.

"No . . . ," Claire mumbled. "We were lost." She was totally unconvincing, but at least she wasn't outright confessing.

"Look," Cookie said, "when we saw you, we were really relieved, because we had finally found our group. We're really sorry that we wandered away, even though it was a total accident, and we promise that we'll stick close by from now on. Can we go back to look at the *Story of We the People* exhibit?

We have to make up for lost time and we don't want to lose this educational opportunity."

There it was again. Doubt. Mrs. Whitaker and Yo-Yo Sub might suspect that the girls had left the museum, but they couldn't prove a thing. Cookie had to stop herself from smiling. This was going to work. She was going to be legendary.

"Ms. Parker," Yo-Yo Sub said, leaning forward and peering at the mostly empty cup of hot chocolate Cookie was still holding. "The Last Drop coffee shop isn't anywhere near here. Where did you get that cup?"

Cookie went blank, and Claire exploded.

JAY WAS VERY, VERY, VERY, VERY, VERY, VERY EX-
cited. "The lovely Daniesha Parker is going to ride
the bus home with us!!!" he bleated. Nick could practically see the exclamation points above Jay's head.
"This is perfect. First we find out that she's safe and sound and
hasn't been abducted by aliens or ruffians, and now she's going
to ride home with us! This is our chance, Nick, old boy."

Was there maybe a way to knock Jay out that would ren-
der him unconscious for the entire trip home without caus-
ing permanent brain damage? Probably not. "Calm down, Jay,"
Nick told him. "She just got separated from her friend, and she
doesn't look like she's in the best mood." He watched as Mrs.
Whitaker and Ms. Zelle marched a blotchy-faced Claire Jones
onto the Auxano bus.

"Poor girl. It must have been so scary for her to be lost in the big city," Jay mused.

Nick looked at him, incredulous. Sometimes it was hard to tell if Jay willed himself to be clueless or if he was actually just genuinely clueless.

"We should probably leave her alone to process her emotions," he said weakly as Jay bounded onto the bus.

Mr. Friend had made sure that Cookie was sitting in the front seat behind the scruffy bus driver, and Jay made a bee-line to the seat directly behind her. Nick swallowed hard and sat next to him.

"Hello, Daniesha," Jay said, leaning over the back of her seat. Cookie Parker turned around and regarded him with a look that could only be described as pure, unadulterated fury. It was a little surprising that her eyes didn't immediately vaporize Jay when he asked, "How are you doing?"

Sit down, Ms. Parker, you're already in enough trouble.
Oh, she's not in trouble! We were just relating to each other as individuals and Daniesha got a little passionate.
If he comes near me again I'm going to get even more passionate.
Mr. Friend, you have to put me back on the other bus.
Fine. Okay. Jay, get your stuff and take it to the other bus.

But... but there's no need! There's plenty of space on this bus.
THAT'S TOTALLY UNFAIR!
I am not dealing with... whatever this is for the next two hours. Cookie, sit down, you're in enough trouble.
I'm sending Jay Carpenter your way. Don't ask.
Can I go with him?
No, Nick, there's not enough room. Yeah, I've got Cookie, Nick, Farshad, and... Martina. Jay's coming over and then we'll be ready to move on out.

FARSHAD LIKED LEARNING NEW WORDS. HE WAS PARticularly fond of *schadenfreude*. It was a German word that basically meant "watching someone else suffer and feeling pretty darned pleased about it." Not that he was particularly proud of himself for being happy about Cookie's troubles. But, seriously, what was he supposed to be feeling? This was the girl who had taken a stupid, racist comment and blown it up into an identity that had brought him nothing but misery for the past two years. It was nice to see her miserable for a change.

Farshad knew Cookie had been the one to let everyone at Deborah Read Middle School know that he was Terror Boy. On the first day of school, he'd seen her with a gaggle of new girls, all of whom were looking over at him and whispering. He had been feeling pretty good, too—new year, new school, all honors classes, a fresh start—but because of Cookie Parker he'd never had the chance to make a good first impression. Girls like Cookie were very good at getting people to listen to them. She had that . . . something, that special power that drew people to her and made them believe whatever she was saying, even when she was telling outright lies. It was especially pleasing to now see her caught in one.

After fuming for a while, Cookie calmed down and stared out her window, and Farshad turned to look out his own window. The sky had become very dark, and traffic on the highway had slowed to a standstill. Mr. Friend was conferring with the frustrated bus driver about possible alternate routes. It was shaping up to be a very long ride home. Farshad put down his study materials and closed his eyes.

COOKIE COULD FEEL TERROR BOY LOOKING AT HER. So creepy. She didn't actually believe that he was a terrorist (get real, he was only twelve), but still, you never knew what kind of person he could turn into. He certainly had what it took to be a terrorist—he was an unpopular loner who gave girls creepy stares. *Gross.* Being on the little bus was the worst.

The bus wasn't moving and Yo-Yo Sub was deep in conversation with the driver, coming up with a plan to get off the highway in order to make better time. Yo-Yo Sub wasn't sure about it, but the bus driver was insistent. He probably wanted to drive them all to an abandoned farmhouse and eat them, or something. Still, it was probably better than sitting in traffic.

No one else seemed bothered when they exited the highway. There was a dark-haired girl a few seats behind Cookie who was scribbling something in a sketchbook—*How is she not carsick?*—and creepy Terror Boy, who had stopped staring at Cookie and was just looking out the window. Jay's dumpy friend was directly behind her. Maybe he was actually Jay's boyfriend or something; they were always hanging out together. They were probably a couple. *Gag.* Cookie made a mental note to tell Addison about it when she got back home. Addison would think it was hilarious and totally tell Izaak. Izaak wouldn't let that juicy tidbit go—he was like a big, dumb shark, and once he had a good bite on his victim he wouldn't let go until they drowned. Cookie smiled. Things were looking up. Jay and his chum really shouldn't have messed with her.

They were off the highway and driving on some sort of back country road, and the darkness and the driving rain made it difficult to see beyond the reach of the headlights of the bus. For a moment Cookie was actually frightened. *Does Weirdo even know where he's going?* Lightning flashed and briefly illuminated the inside of the bus. Yo-Yo Sub was biting his thumbnail and Jay's friend looked a little queasy. If he was going to barf, that would be just perfect. Worst bus ride ever.

The bus lurched, and for a moment Cookie wondered if she would be the one to throw up—it felt as if the bus were falling onto its side. As Cookie was flung out of her seat it occurred to her that the bus actually was flipping over, and that there would be no time for puking. She instinctively raised her arms to cover her head, and that was when she heard the unfamiliar sound of her own screaming.

Everything was wrong. Cookie saw Terror Boy get tossed across her field of vision like a rag doll and then her head slammed against something hard and sharp. The bus was still moving, and she could see a wave of dirt hitting the windshield. Were they going to be buried alive?

Were they even still alive?

WET. NICK WAS VERY WET. NO, WAIT, IT WAS THE ground. The ground was very wet. The wet ground was making him wet. Also, the rain falling on top of the wet ground was making him wet. A very wet blade of grass was sticking directly into his right nostril, but Nick wasn't moving. Could he move? Nick could feel things, like the mud seeping into the front of his shirt and the rain pounding on his back. Could he see? Thunder boomed overhead, much too close for comfort. He could definitely hear things. Was that a horse? Nick opened his eyes.

He was lying in the muddy grass about fifteen feet from the bus, which was overturned in the ditch on the side of the road. Lightning flashed, and for a split second he could see a figure near the bus. Nick stretched out his wet arms to the guy, trying to call out to him. "Hey . . ." His voice sounded tiny and weak. Nick put his palms on the rain-soaked ground and tried to push himself up. The mud made a disgusting sucking sound as it reluctantly released the bulk of his body. "Hey!" he called out again, a little bit louder. He struggled to his feet.

Dizzy. *Did I hit my head?* It looked to Nick like he'd been flung fifteen feet from the rolling bus. *Of course I hit my head.* But his head didn't hurt. Was he dead? *Maybe I'm dead. Do dead people get this soggy?* Probably not. Nick hadn't been to church since his dad died, but it seemed doubtful that his jeans would be this caked with mud in the afterlife. Also, if he was dead, he'd be seeing his dad. No, for better or worse, Nick was alive.

Nick tested his legs. Walking was definitely not a problem. He began to slog through the soggy field to the ditch, where he saw someone who appeared to be wearing a straw hat struggling to open the back door of the bus.

A gruesome thought occurred to him. *Oh no.* What if there were dead bodies? What if he only lived because he'd been lucky enough to be thrown from the bus? *And how, exactly, was I thrown from the bus?* None of the windows had been open and the bus looked intact. *Weird.* Nick stopped moving forward. Where was he, even?

"COME!" Hat Guy had spotted him. Nick ran to the back of the bus and grabbed the emergency handle, which Hat Guy had somehow not figured out how to work. The door swung open and the smell of gas filled the air, along with some other sort of pungent chemical that Nick couldn't place. He and Hat Guy started to cough.

The first person they saw inside was Cookie Parker. She was trying to make her way toward him and her eyes were wide with fear. Nick saw a small stream of blood running down the side of her head. "WE HAVE TO GET EVERYONE OFF THE BUS," she screamed, and pointed to a brown-haired girl who was passed out near the open door.

"Are you sure we should move her?" Nick yelped.

The passed-out girl moaned. Cookie looked at her. "YES!" she yelled.

Nick found himself momentarily annoyed. When had Cookie Parker become a doctor? Yet there he was, climbing into the chemical-stank bus and grabbing the girl's arms to pull her out of her seat.

Hat Guy put his hand on Nick's arm to stop him. "No no," he said. "I get her. I'm stronger."

For the first time, Nick took a good look at the stranger. He was tall, but he looked young, only a few years older than Nick. He was dressed in black pants and a white shirt with no buttons on it. Nick recognized the style. The Amish boy gently pushed past Nick and Cookie and lifted the girl up like she weighed nothing.

The brown-haired girl moaned again and opened her eyes. They were glowing bright yellow. Cookie let out a small, sharp shriek.

FARSHAD SENSED OTHER PEOPLE MOVING NEAR HIM, but he didn't open his eyes. Everything hurt and he was pretty sure that seeing his surroundings wasn't going to make him feel any better.

"Hey." Farshad felt a hand shaking his shoulder. He opened one eye and saw a chubby kid with glasses who was dripping water onto him. "Hey, are you okay?" the kid asked. "Can you move?"

Farshad blinked a few times, trying to get his eyes to adjust to the low light. He tried to stretch and found that he was lying on his side but could move. "Yeah," he said, "I think so."

"We're getting out of the bus." The kid knelt down next to him and began fumbling with his safety belt. Through Farshad's fuzziness some small part of him felt a pang of sadness. He couldn't remember the last time that someone his own age had talked to him like he was a human being. He gently pushed the kid's hand away and unbuckled his own safety belt.

"NICK!" a female voice screamed. The kid spun around. Through the darkness Farshad could make out Cookie Parker's features. She had blood on her face and she looked frightened. "NICK, I CAN'T TELL IF YO—IF MR. FRIEND IS BREATHING."

"Are you okay here?" Nick asked Farshad. He nodded and Nick clumsily made his way over some seats to where Cookie Parker was shrieking. Farshad got up, grabbed his backpack, and climbed over the seats to join them.

It didn't look good. Mr. Friend was passed out and his leg was pinned at a weird angle underneath one of the seats.

"Okay," Nick said. "Okay okay okay. We have to find a way to get him . . . unstuck."

"How?" Cookie asked. "He looks all twisted and gross. Are we totally sure he's alive?"

Nick climbed over a seat and put his ear near Mr. Friend's mouth. "He's breathing. Can we move this seat?" he asked, gesturing to the twisted piece of metal that was crushing the substitute teacher's right leg.

"Sure, no problem." Cookie rolled her eyes as Nick tried to crawl under another seat to see if there was a way to move it. "Let me just grab my portable Jaws of Life out of my bag." She began to cough.

"I don't think we should wait," Nick mumbled. "It smells really weird in here."

For the first time, it occurred to Farshad that maybe his dizziness had more to do with the chemical and gas smells than it did with hitting his head. Nick grabbed the bottom of the seat and wheezed as he tried to lift it. "A little help?"

Cookie shot Farshad a look as if to say, *Is he serious?* Through his fog, Farshad felt a surge of anger, because this was Cookie Parker, and Cookie Parker did not get to share knowing looks with him. "Move," he said, pushing past her and grabbing the other end of the seat. It really wasn't that heavy, but the metal made a horrible screeching sound as he lifted it up. It was so loud he could feel it in his teeth. He tossed the seat aside and it landed with a dull crash. "Get him," Farshad grunted to Cookie and Nick, who stared at him for a moment before each took hold of one of Mr. Friend's arms and dragged him to the back of the bus. Farshad followed them out into the rain, where a strange boy was standing, staring at a cell phone.

It was only a matter of seconds before Farshad was drenched. They hauled Mr. Friend about thirty feet down the road to where a brown-haired girl sat clutching her backpack. "Is he dead?" she asked, looking at Mr. Friend.

"He's breathing." Nick wheezed under the weight of the substitute teacher as they roughly set him down on the pavement. Mr. Friend let out a small groan. "Any reception?" Nick asked the stranger, who looked like he was in his teens.

"I'm sorry, I can't make it go," he said somewhat helplessly.

Cookie snatched the phone away from him and held it up. "I got bars," she said, dialing 911.

A wave of dizziness hit Farshad and he sank to the wet pavement next to the brown-haired girl. She was using her rain jacket to protect her backpack, but the rest of her body was soaking wet. "Are you okay?" he asked her.

"I'm very cold," she said, her teeth chattering as she hugged her things to her chest. "And also soggy." She looked at him with light blue eyes. "You don't look very good."

"I'm okay," he said tiredly, but his head felt light and his eyelids were heavy.

"Should we put him in my buggy?" he heard the teenager ask. He had a strange accent.

Farshad looked up and saw a horse looking down at him. That was new. Behind the horse was a covered buggy.

"I don't know if we should keep moving him." Nick said. Lightning momentarily illuminated the sky and Mr. Friend whimpered without opening his eyes.

"My farm isn't far from here," the boy said. "I can go and get help." He climbed into the buggy and set off down the road.

"He seemed nice," the green-eyed girl said to Farshad. His head was spinning.

Flashing red and blue lights of emergency vehicles appeared in the distance, and Farshad felt a measure of relief. He closed his eyes and felt his body hit the wet ground.

THE EMERGENCY ROOM AT MUELLERSVILLE MEMO-
rial seemed really loud to Cookie. It was probably
just a symptom of the mild concussion that the doctors suspected she had, but the noise made it hard
for her to think. She wanted very badly for her mother to come.

Closing her eyes didn't help to block out the noise. Everyone in the hospital seemed to be thinking aloud, which hurt
Cookie's head and was also just very annoying. *"Left . . . another left . . . right,"* one female voice said. Cookie opened her
eyes to see a woman wearing scrubs weaving her way through
the hallways. *"Where's the exit? I swear I came through here,"*
another guy said. It was like they couldn't think without opening their mouths. Didn't they understand that there were traumatized and potentially concussed people trying to get a little
rest?

Cookie couldn't stop thinking about the girl's eyes. It wasn't
real, Cookie told herself. It was a trick of the lighting, or the
lightning, or stress, or the result of a mild concussion. After all,
when she'd gone back to get her phone, the girl's eyes had been
some perfectly unremarkable shade of brown. So it was all in
Cookie's slightly busted-up head, right?

Only, it wasn't. She was absolutely positive that Nick had
seen it, too. His mouth had dropped open, and they'd shared
the same astonished *WHAT THE???* look. She knew that he'd

seen what she'd seen and she knew that he knew that she knew that he'd seen it.

"Second left . . ." Cookie heard her mother coming and sank back into her pillow, relieved. She'd deal with Nick and all this freaky yellow-eye stuff later.

**N**ICK DID NOT LIKE HOSPITALS, FOR OBVIOUS REA- sons, but when the doctors heard that he'd been thrown fifteen feet from the bus, they weren't particularly eager to release him. He had tried to explain to them that, really, he felt fine, and that being kept in a hospital bed was going to terrify his mom (she REALLY didn't like hospitals), but they wouldn't let him out and wouldn't give him back his soggy clothes. Nick just had to sit and wait for the inevitable Mom Freak-out.

To her credit, Nick's mom kept it together for, oh, maybe four seconds. "Hi, sweetie," she said as she came into the room with his aunt Molly right behind her. His mother looked wild-eyed and frazzled, and his aunt's strained expression revealed that his mom was gripping Molly's hand tightly enough for it to hurt.

"Hi, Mom," Nick said. "Did you bring clothes?"

You'd think that saying something simple like "Did you bring clothes?" would not hit any emotional triggers, but Nick probably could have said something like "So, how about them Phillies?" or "My hovercraft is full of eels," and his mom still would have burst into sobs. His dad probably would have smiled and muttered, "So predictable."

"Look, Angie, he's fine," Molly said gently, using her right hand to rub life back into her left one.

"Really, Mom, I'm okay," Nick said.

"You are never getting on a bus again!" Nick's mom howled, and Molly and Nick stared at her until she calmed down. "Okay, okay," she said, wiping her red nose with the tissue Molly handed her. "Okay, you can get on a bus. That may have been a little extreme."

"I'm fine, Mom," Nick said as she clutched his hand. "Did you bring clothes?" he asked again. Molly held out a plastic bag, and he wondered how exactly he was going to get his mom and aunt out of the room long enough to change.

"Excuse me, Mr. Gross?" A uniformed police officer stood in the doorway. "We'd like to ask you a few questions about the accident."

"Sure," Nick said. *Mr. Gross.* Weird. The officer pulled up a chair and took out a little notebook. Nick told him about how he'd woken up in the field and seen the guy (the driver, he guessed) fleeing the scene, and how he'd made his way back to help the Amish kid and Cookie get everyone else off the bus. He didn't mention the girl's eyes turning bright yellow or Farshad Rajavi lifting up a bolted-down bus seat like it was made of cardboard—either of which would have made Nick seem like he'd been hit pretty hard on the head. His mom didn't need that. Also, the officer never asked anything like "And did you by chance notice if any of your bus mates were suddenly in possession of crazy-weird superpowers?"

There had to be a reasonable explanation. The girl's yellow-looking eyes were probably just a trick of the light, and Farshad must have been full of adrenaline to pull up that seat, which would explain why he went unconscious right before the ambulance arrived. *That's what happens to people who have an adrenaline surge, right? They collapse when it's over? Jay would know.* Nick made a mental note to check on Farshad before leaving the hospital (after he had pants on). Sure, everyone called Farshad "Terror Boy" and pretty much hated his guts, but it was sort of a personal rule of Nick's to always be nice to people in hospitals.

FARSHAD FELT FLOATY. THE DOCTORS HAD TOLD HIS parents that he had a concussion and would have to spend the night at the hospital for observation. His father had brought a pile of books for Farshad to read so that he wouldn't get bored or watch too much television, but the thought of reading was laughable. The doctors had him on some sort of pain medication that made the words swim in front of his eyes.

His mother had wanted to stay in the hospital room with him, but after the police officer took his statement (*bus crashed; we got out of bus*) and the school principal had come for a quick visit to see how he was doing, Farshad just wanted to be left alone. Plus, who can sleep with their mom trying to get comfortable in a hospital chair next to them? It took a while for his father to convince her to leave so that Farshad could get some rest.

After they were gone, Farshad tried to watch some television, but there wasn't much on. It turned out that the idea of watching television in bed was a lot more exciting than actually watching television in bed. There was a knock at the door and he turned off the set.

"Hey, how are you doing?" It was Nick, the chubby kid from the bus.

"Hey," Farshad said. His voice sounded weird in his head. "They have me on medication. You?"

Nick was dressed in regular clothes. "Nah, I'm fine, they're letting me out. How long do you have to be here?"

"They'll let me out tomorrow morning," Farshad said. "They think I have a slight concussion and they want to keep me under observation."

"Lame," Nick said, pulling up the visitor's chair and sitting down without an invitation. "But otherwise you're okay? No broken bones or anything?"

"No, I'm fine," Farshad said. His tongue felt sluggish. "You?"

"Not a scratch. The doctors say it's a miracle, because I was thrown so far from the bus."

"I don't believe in miracles," Farshad said. He really didn't.

"No, me neither," Nick said. "I guess I'm just lucky."

Farshad's head started to pound. He wasn't feeling particularly generous. "I don't believe in luck, either."

Nick chuckled. "Then I guess I've discovered a new talent for getting safely thrown out of moving vehicles. I wonder if I could somehow parlay this incredible skill into a career?"

He was a weird kid. "You could maybe be a stuntman?" Farshad suggested, hoping that maybe Nick would start by jumping out the hospital window and leaving him alone.

Nick smiled. "That makes sense, what with my action star physique."

Farshad understood that Nick was being friendly, but he just didn't feel like taking the weird kid's charity. Anyway, was he supposed to acknowledge that Nick was a little fat by laughing, or maybe lie and tell him that he looked great? Farshad chose neither, closing his mouth and staring down at the television remote in his hand.

After a few awkward seconds Nick got up. "Well, my mom's waiting," he mumbled. "Guess I should go and let you rest. Feel better soon."

There was another knock on the door, and Ms. Zelle poked her head into the room. Farshad immediately felt self-conscious of the fact that he was only wearing a flimsy hospital gown. He was weirdly grateful for Nick's presence, even though the kid's face had become much, much pinker.

"Hey, guys," Ms. Zelle said quietly, coming into the room. "Mind if I come in?"

"Sure." Farshad gestured to the seat that Nick had just vacated.

"I was just leaving," Nick said, moving to the door.

"No, no stay," Ms. Zelle said, settling in. "Don't leave on my account. I wanted to know how you are both doing."

"Fine," Farshad and Nick said in unison.

Ms. Zelle looked at them with a worried expression on her small, delicate face. "Now, I'm sure that's not true," she said, "but if you're being brave, I'll just have to believe that." She looked down at her phone for a moment. "I came here to see how Ry—how Mr. Friend was doing, but I can't seem to find his room, so I thought I'd check on you. I don't suppose you've seen him, have you?"

"No," Farshad and Nick said, again at the same time.

"Of course not, you're too busy getting better." Ms. Zelle smiled at both of them as she stood up. "Okay, well, I'm going to keep looking. Feel better soon, both of you, and remember, I'll be in school if you ever need to take a break or talk about anything. Sometimes being in an accident can have some weird residual effects on a person."

"Like what?" Nick asked as Farshad said, "Thanks, bye." Ms. Zelle smiled one last time and left the room. Nick shuffled out after her. Farshad leaned back, shut his eyes, and immediately regretted not thanking Nick for coming, as well. It really was a decent thing to do. But he was tired and his head hurt and he just wasn't used to kids his own age being decent.

NICK FELL ASLEEP ALMOST AS SOON AS HIS HEAD HIT the pillow. It was pretty late and it had been a long day. The next thing he knew there was sunlight in his eyes and Jay was staring down at him.

"Dude," Nick groaned, "are you watching me sleep? Because: weird and not okay."

"I'm not watching you sleep, I'm waiting for you to wake up. Are you awake now?"

"Either I'm awake or I'm having a really terrible dream about you opening my window shades and not letting me sleep."

Jay pinched himself. "I felt that, so I'm awake." Then he pinched Nick's arm.

"Ow!"

"Clearly you felt that, so you're awake, too. Sorry, I just had to be sure."

"Do we need to have another conversation about boundaries?" Nick groggily pushed himself up to a sitting position. He still felt grubby from yesterday evening's quick nap in the muddy field. He looked at Jay, who was absentmindedly nibbling the cuticles around his nails. "I think I need a shower," Nick said.

Jay leaned forward and sniffed him. "You do. I'm going to have some coffee with Angela and when you get out I want to hear all about what happened last night."

"I don't think my mom is going to give you coffee."

Jay dismissed Nick's comment with a wave of his hand. "Nonsense. We are civilized individuals and it is morning, which is when civilized individuals sit down with their morning mugs of coffee. See you in fifteen." He bounced out of the room. There was no way that Nick's mom was going to purposefully caffeinate Jay, but his confidence never failed to astound.

After his shower Nick came downstairs to find Jay and his mom engrossed in whatever was on her laptop. They had mugs in front of them, but after a brief moment of disbelief Nick saw that Jay's was filled with orange juice. This didn't stop Jay from reaching for Nick's mom's mug of black coffee. She batted his hand away without looking up from the screen.

"Nicholas, my good man!" Jay exclaimed as Nick came into the kitchen. "You're famous." He stole a deep gulp from Nick's mom's mug as she stood up to give Nick a tight good-morning hug.

Over her shoulder, Nick could see Jay's eyes bugging out from the burning heat of the coffee. He stifled a laugh. "Excuse me?"

Jay swallowed quickly and turned the laptop around to show Nick an article on the local news site. It was a short piece about the crash, but no names were mentioned.

"Somebody start inking the deal for the movie rights," Nick muttered as he poured himself a glass of water.

"But that's not all!" Jay said, his eyes glowing. "Principal Jacobs herself called this morning to ask how you were!"

Nick looked at his mom, who nodded with a smile.

"Aaaaaand," Jay went on, opening another window on the computer, "you've made The Hammer's home page!" The Hammer was a local conspiracy theorist with a blog called *The Daily Whut?* that Jay was obsessed with. Nick used to read the blog all the time ("Muellersville School Board: What Happened to the Funding for Earthquake Preparedness???") until he realized that The Hammer was just another person making up stories because he wanted people's attention (or Jay's attention, because Nick couldn't imagine anyone else actually taking the time). He sat down to read.

When he was done, Nick looked up to see both his mom and Jay looking at him expectantly. "What?" he asked.

"What happened to the driver?" Jay bleated.

"I don't know," Nick said, and told them what he'd seen, even though his mom had already heard the whole story the night before. Jay was rapt.

"So an Amish man helped you out! That didn't even make it into the article! We totally have the inside scoop! And you actually worked with Daniesha to SAVE LIVES," he said in a voice that managed to be dreamy *and* loud. "How did she smell?"

"I was genuinely not paying attention." Nick looked at the

clock. "Come on, we have to go. We're going to be late for the bus."

"Oh, no no no," his mom said, "you haven't had any breakfast, and no buses for you today. I'm driving you to school."

"Mom, I'm fine . . ."

She gave Nick her *Resistance is futile* look and he slunk back into his chair as she put frozen waffles into the toaster oven.

Jay was giddy. "This is going to be AMAZING," he said. "You're a celebrity, and we're getting chauffeured to school!"

Nick heard his mom suppress a giggle. Jay was crazy, but you had to love the little nutball.

COOKIE'S MOM WANTED HER TO STAY HOME FROM school, but there was no way—her friends would want to see her to make sure she was okay. Also, she kind of wanted to see the look on Mr. Friend's face when she showed up with the bandage on her head, which Cookie never would have had if he hadn't insisted on putting her in harm's way. She was pretty sure that she was off the hook for the whole temporarily-leaving-the-field-trip thing— Principal Jacobs hadn't even mentioned it when she'd called to check on her.

Cookie also felt a strong urge to talk to Nick about that girl's freaky-eye-color situation. It would be tricky, because of course she didn't actually want anyone to *see* her talking to Nick, but Cookie figured that there would be some point in the day when he'd be alone.

Cookie's stepfather drove her to school. George was usually okay, but he was doing that thing where he felt like he had to mention every turn he was taking. "Make a right here . . . Turn onto Lombard . . . Should I take Pleasant Street? I'm going to hit a light if I do . . . Oh, we have the time, let's turn onto Pleasant . . ." He was giving her a headache. She turned the volume up on the radio and tried to ignore him.

The front entrance seemed especially loud, so by the time the warning bell rang, Cookie was beginning to wonder if coming in had been such a hot idea. She felt an arm around her shoulders.

"Oh my god, I can't believe you're okay!" Addison was hugging her tight. She pulled back and looked at Cookie, her face blanching at the sight of the small bandage on her friend's forehead. "Holy crap, shouldn't you be in, like, the hospital?"

"The doctors said it's just a little cut." Cookie's voice sounded quieter than she wanted it to. She took a deep breath. "Does everyone know about the accident?"

"It was on the news last night!" Addison took Cookie's arm and began steering her toward their homeroom. "My mom saw it and I immediately texted you—I guess you didn't get my text? So I was freaking out and I texted Izaak and he didn't know anything, so we thought about texting someone else who was on the bus, but seriously, was anyone else even *on* that bus?"

"Hardly," Cookie said. She thought for a second about telling her that Terror Boy had been there, but Addison started chattering about how she and Izaak were so worried, and Cookie didn't have the energy to interrupt her.

Things were quieter in homeroom even though absolutely everybody kept coming up to Cookie to ask what had happened and to look at her bandage and give her hugs and tell her that they were so glad that she was okay. Principal Jacobs poked her head into the room to see how she was, and even

Mrs. Whitaker seemed happy to see her and appeared to have forgotten all about the previous day's transgressions.

"Okay, okay, settle down," Mrs. Whitaker said after the final bell. Everyone sat in their seats, but Cookie could tell they were still looking at her. She cocked her head and pulled her hair back, away from the bandage a little, so people could get a better look. That was when she saw the girl with the yellow eyes.

She was sitting closer to the back of the room. Cookie had never noticed she was in that class—she'd never really even noticed her at the school before. The girl had been doodling something in her sketchbook and now looked up at Cookie. She gave a little wave.

And her eyes turned from a perfectly normal brown to a distinctly not-normal green.

**S**TAYING HOME FROM SCHOOL WAS NEVER AS FUN as you thought it was going to be. Sure, it was great not to be at school, but that just meant that your mom or dad had to stay home with you, so it's not like you were going to get away with watching a lot of television or anything. And if they did let you watch television, they were going to be right there, so you kind of felt pressured to pick a documentary about font types or something other than a movie about ninjas kicking ass. Farshad was sure there were kids who didn't care what their parents thought about what they chose to watch on TV, but his parents were some of the only people who still liked him, so he wanted their approval.

His father had lent Farshad his laptop, so he opened it up instead and did a search for the accident while his mother fussed over him. There wasn't much information—mostly just a short article on *Lancaster Online* about how the bus went off the road. Farshad hadn't read about the driver disappearing (weird), and some nut blogger went on and on about that, as if there were something more to it than just some cowardly jerk who had probably been drinking or something running away after he crashed a school bus full of kids. Or maybe the guy hit his head and stumbled away and was currently lying facedown in some ditch. Maybe he was trampled by the Amish guy's horse.

Neither of the articles mentioned anyone's names, which

was kind of too bad, because Farshad had actually helped get Mr. Friend off the bus, and having some positive press out there would be a plus. He also couldn't find out from the articles if anyone else had stayed home from school. That Nick kid had seemed to be doing okay, but Cookie had been bleeding from a head wound. Whatever. She was probably back at school, because the whole place would fall apart or something if she was absent for a day.

Farshad was pretty sure that all the adults were just going to conveniently forget that she skipped out on the field trip. There's no way they were going to discipline someone who had just been in a major accident.

Some people *were* just lucky.

COOKIE FIGURED THAT ONE NICE THING ABOUT BEing black was that, when she saw the weird girl change her eye color, she didn't blanche. She was pretty sure that all of the blood had left her face, but she knew no one could tell.

Still. Cookie felt dizzy. Because EYES AREN'T SUPPOSED TO DO THAT. She turned away from the girl and raised her hand.

"Yes, Daniesha?"

"May I go to the bathroom? I'm not feeling great."

Mrs. Whitaker looked worried. "Perhaps if you're not feeling well you should head straight to the nurse," she said, looking at the bandage on Cookie's head.

No, because if I go to the nurse they're going to send me home and I don't need to be sent home, Cookie thought. *I need to find that dippy kid Nick and confirm what we saw so that I know I'm not going completely insane.* "I think I just need to splash some water on my face," she said. "If I don't feel better after that I'll go to the nurse?"

Mrs. Whitaker pursed her lips. No teacher liked to give a kid an open-ended hallway pass. "Just sign Mr. Friend's get-well card first," she said, bringing it over to Cookie before writing out the pass.

In the hallway, Cookie actually did feel better. She was now away from the yellow-eyed girl, but she was also away from everyone, and for the first time since she woke up that morning, Cookie felt like she could breathe.

"Cookie!" Now Ms. Zelle was coming down the hallway toward her. Fantastic. "Are you all right?"

Don't let her see that you're losing it, Cookie told herself. *Stay cool.* "Hey, Ms. Zelle."

The science teacher was looking worriedly at Cookie's head. "I'm a little surprised to see you in school today."

"The doctors said it was fine," Cookie told her, trying to sound nonchalant. "Besides, the exam is next week. Gotta keep studying."

Ms. Zelle smiled. That woman just loved statewide exams, probably because she still got paid to teach when all she was actually doing was reading magazines while the tests were being taken. "Of course, of course," she said, "but don't push yourself too hard, okay? And get plenty of rest. Rest is good for the brain." Ms. Zelle tapped her index finger to her own temple.

"Sure, Ms. Zelle." Cookie smiled back and turned to walk purposefully down the hallway toward the bathroom. As soon as she rounded the corner, she allowed herself to exhale.

Nick Gross. Where would a kid like that have homeroom? She couldn't just start knocking on doors, looking for nerds.

But wait. Where did nerds hang out between classes? Cookie always spent her time near her locker, where people would come to talk to her, or in the girls' bathroom, if she needed to freshen up or pee. *I need to think like a nerd,* Cookie thought. *Where would I be if I were a great big loser with no friends who should probably just hide away until high school graduation?*

She made a beeline to the staircase farthest away from the gymnasium. Cookie knew that she had to get there before homeroom ended. She didn't want to deal with another crowded hallway.

JAY HAD DISCOVERED THE UNDERSTEPS BEFORE THEY had even gotten to middle school. He'd insisted on coming in to school the week before it started so that he could get a lay of the land. "We can't be stumbling AROUND like a bunch of sixth grade know-nothings!" he had explained to Nick. "Everyone will think that we're complete IGNORAMUSES!" Nick didn't know if people thought that they looked like ignoramuses, but there was no avoiding looking like sixth grade know-nothings, because at that point they clearly were in sixth grade and knew absolutely nothing. But Jay discovered the Understeps, and Nick had admitted that it was pretty cool. It was this little space underneath the back stairs where a couple of people could be without anyone noticing, and whoever had used the Understeps before them had left a little message carved into the cinderblock: *Nolite te bastardes carborundorum*. Jay had memorized it and looked it up on the Internet, and it was Latin for "Don't let the bastards grind you down." Not that Jay ever paid any mind to anyone trying to grind him down, but Nick did, and he was really fond of the carved message. Sometimes he wondered who wrote it, and how long ago, and how they were doing. *Well*, he hoped.

Nick would come to the Understeps between classes to listen to a song on his iPod for a minute without worrying that a hall monitor would catch him and confiscate his music, or to meet up with Jay to play cards or something during lunch if he didn't feel like dealing with the cafeteria. Nick had just put his earbuds in when Cookie appeared.

"Nick, we need to talk."

He blinked at her. Seeing Cookie in the Understeps was like seeing a teacher at the movies—it just didn't seem right for that person to exist in that space.

Nick took his earbuds out. Cookie had a bandage on her head and a weird look on her face. "Um, okay," he said. "How are you feeling?"

"I feel weird, Nick," Cookie said in a tone that was both accusatory and exasperated, as if it were his fault that she felt weird and he was stupid for not knowing that. Jeez, she really could make a person feel small.

"I'm . . . sorry?"

"Well, don't you feel a little weird?" She was kind of terrifying.

"I . . . I guess I feel a little weird. But I'm okay, you know, I didn't hurt my head or anything."

"It's not my head wound that's making me feel weird, Nick. It's what we saw yesterday. Don't you think that what we saw was a little weird, Nick?"

Had someone told Nick yesterday that he'd be having a conversation in the Understeps with Cookie Parker about some sort of shared hallucination, he would have thought they were totally wackadoo. He wasn't sure if he even wanted to talk about what he had seen on the bus, let alone if he wanted to talk about it with her. The whole situation was too alien. He froze.

"Well?" Cookie asked. "Did you see something weird or not?" She had her hands on her hips and was impatiently tapping her fingernails on her belt. She seemed annoyed, but she looked . . . she actually looked a little scared.

"Yes," Nick admitted. "I saw something weird."

KNEW IT," COOKIE SAID.

"Daniesha!" Nobody called Cookie that. She looked up. Had Nick somehow told The Shrimp that she was here? No, impossible, he hadn't known that she was coming. They just hung out here together because no one else wanted to be around them. Cookie certainly didn't want to be around them. Particularly The Shrimp.

Get it together, girl. Just because Cookie wasn't feeling like herself was no reason The Shrimp should be spared her wrath. If Cookie had had superpowers, lasers would have been shooting out of her eyes and incinerating him on the spot. She might not be at the top of her game, but Cookie could still cut with a look.

"Daniesha, my delicate black orchid, let me see your wound." Did laser-beam eyes mean nothing to this kid?

"If you step any closer, so help me, I will drop you," Cookie growled. She had never actually committed any acts of deliberate violence, but a secluded stairwell seemed like a good place to start.

The Shrimp held his shrimpy hands up. "I understand, I'm not a medical professional. But that doesn't mean that I don't have a gentle, healing touch."

"Are you kidding me?" Cookie heard herself getting louder despite her aching head. "ARE YOU SERIOUS?" She whipped

around to Nick, and trained her laser beams on him. "IS HE
SERIOUS?"

And just like that, Nick disappeared. Sort of.

**NE MOMENT SHE WAS SCREAMING AT HIM, AND** the next . . . nothing. No sounds were coming out of her mouth. Cookie was just staring at Nick with her eyes wide and her mouth hanging open, and Jay was next to her, looking equally shocked. They stood there, eyes locked on him.

"Um . . . hi," Nick said after what was at least a full minute of slack-jawed silence. The late bell rang, but no one moved. "Shouldn't we get going?"

"Did you see that?" Cookie asked, still staring.

"See what?" Nick asked.

"I saw it," Jay said. Nick had never seen him look that way before. Jay looked serious.

"Saw what?" Nick asked. He felt very strange, as if a small, cold breeze was blowing on the back of his neck.

"So . . . say, Nick, old man. How long have you been able to teleport?"

"Excuse me?"

"How long, exactly, have you been able to change locations in a split second without moving?" Jay asked. "Is this a new thing? Because I don't think I've seen you do it before."

It was Nick's turn to stare at Jay. This had to be another one of his crazy fantasies. Nick looked at Cookie. "Ignore him."

"I think you should answer him," she whispered.

"What? Why?"

"I JUST SAW YOU DO IT!" Cookie half screamed, half bleated.

Silence.

"HE DID IT AGAIN! DID YOU SEE THAT?"

Jay looked very pale. "I saw it."

Nick was about to tell Jay that he was clearly delusional, but he was interrupted by the loud boom of the first explosion.

THEY RAN TOGETHER. UNDER ANY OTHER CIRCUM-
stance, being seen anywhere near Jay Carpenter
and Nick Gross in public was pretty unthinkable for
Cookie, but it seemed like *unthinkable* was quickly
becoming the word of the day.

As they bolted toward the glowing-red EMERGENCY EXIT
sign, Nick disappeared and reappeared twice. "STOP THAT!"
Cookie screamed at him.

"I CAN'T!" he yelled over the sounds of the fire alarm, disappearing again and immediately showing up slightly to the
left of where he had just been.

"DO SOMETHING!" Cookie screamed to Jay, who immediately jumped on Nick's back.

"WHAT ARE YOU DOING???" Nick roared.

"RUN!" Jay squeaked, clinging to Nick for dear life as
they all bolted out the door and headed for the small hill that
overlooked the sports fields. Students were streaming out of
the building while teachers tried to keep everyone calm. A
huge plume of dark gray smoke was rising up from behind
the school. Cookie looked at Nick. He hadn't blinked out once
since Jay had jumped on his back.

Nick was turning red. "Can't . . . go . . . farther . . ." he
wheezed, dumping Jay on the ground and immediately disappearing again.

When he rematerialized, Cookie grabbed his arm and looked at Jay. "If one of us isn't holding on to him, he'll disappear again!"

"ON IT!" Jay yelled, jumping back on top of Nick, who stumbled and fell and dragged them all down with him.

Oh dear god. Cookie was lying in the wet grass with Nick Gross and Jay Carpenter. What if Izaak saw her? Or Claire? She knew that she could never say, "That wasn't me, that was some other black girl who looked exactly like me—you know, the other black girl?" because there were no other black girls in the school. There was an Indian girl, Harshita Singh, but only the dumbest, most nearsighted racist would confuse Cookie with her. She untangled herself but stayed low to the ground, hoping against hope that things were too chaotic down on the field for anyone to notice her. "Don't. Let. Him. Go," she ordered Jay.

"Yes, my queen," Jay responded, pinning Nick to the ground. Cookie gagged.

"Get off me!" Nick groaned.

"No," Jay said. "I think the beautiful and intelligent Daniesha is right. I think that if someone is holding on to you, you can't . . . do whatever it is that you're doing."

"Holding on to someone and tackling them to the ground are two different things!" Nick said, panting.

"Right," Jay said, looking at Cookie. "Hold his hand."

"Ew, no," Cookie said. Nick looked hurt. "No offense," she added somewhat lamely.

"Fine, *I'll* hold his hand." Jay grabbed Nick's hand while rolling off of him. They got awkwardly to their feet. "Pleased to make your acquaintance!" Jay giggled, pumping Nick's hand.

"And how do you do?" Nick laughed.

Cookie stared at them. Then looked down at the students and teachers still filing out onto the field. The thought of joining the larger group made Cookie feel dizzy. They were already so loud.

"Daniesha?" Jay asked. He looked worried. "Are you all right?"

She could hear them all buzzing inside her head, talking about how to get out of the field and back to their houses, and how to get back into the school and to their classes, and which would be the best way to sneak out . . . It was so loud. Cookie put her hands over her ears to muffle the noise, but there was no difference. She spotted Mrs. Whitaker down on the field. Standing next to her was the girl with the yellow eyes. The girl was too far away to see her eye color, but she was looking right at Cookie.

Nick came up to Cookie, dragging Jay with him. She saw him mouth her name but couldn't hear him over the noise from everyone below.

Suddenly she heard a very loud voice saying, *I have to get to the back steps.* Her hands were clasped firmly over her ears but it was like the voice was right by her ear. *I have to find her. I have to take the hallway near the theater and get out where no one can see me. I have to find that emergency exit.*

Cookie turned to point at the emergency exit door they had just used. "Someone's coming," she said. Two seconds later Mr. Friend, wild-eyed, limping, and wearing a long jacket over a hospital gown, burst out. He saw them immediately.

"YOU!" he yelled, pointing at Nick, Jay, and Cookie. Behind them a tree burst into flames.

RUN.

As the ball of fire erupted in the trees at the edge of the schoolyard, the orderly lines of students below immediately melted into a screaming, running swarm. Cookie took off toward the forest that bordered the soccer field and Jay and Nick followed, not bothering to look back to see what had become of Mr. Friend.

Nick fell as soon as they hit the hill, losing his grip on Jay's bony little hand. As Nick tumbled he knew that he was blinking in and out. That's what it felt like—blinking. Blink, and he was a little farther to his left than he'd been before. Blink, and it happened again.

"COME ON!" Cookie roared. She grabbed Nick's hand and dragged him up to a standing position. Jay quickly grabbed his other hand as they set off at a run. Most of the other students

were running toward the main road, away from the row of flaming trees, but Cookie veered to the left and dragged them toward a girl who was standing alone and watching the chaos. Cookie let go of Nick and grabbed the girl. "You're coming with us," she said.

The girl with the bright yellow eyes was now part of their group. She smiled at Cookie as they ran.

THE DAILY WHUT?

WHAT'S GOING ON??? Dear Hammerfans, in the past three hours there have been FOUR REPORTED EXPLOSIONS in Muellersville. There was an explosion in a parked car outside of the Muellersville hospital, another in a parked car on Denby Street, yet another IN THE PARKING LOT OF DEBORAH READ MIDDLE SCHOOL, and YET ANOTHER when a line of trees caught on fire . . . ON THE OTHER SIDE OF THE SCHOOL.

Now, some would say that we have a DEADLY ARSONIST in our midst (although, to be clear, no one has actually died . . . YET). The Hammer thinks it's something even more nefarious—what if it's MORE THAN ONE PERSON? Why haven't we heard from Principal Jacobs? After all, it's her school and the trees near her school that are on fire. Isn't anyone willing to hold her feet to the flames? NOT LITERALLY. But we need some answers, and we need them before the truth is too hot to handle.

Keep asking questions,
The Hammer

COOKIE WASN'T COMPLETELY SURE WHY SHE'D grabbed the girl; then again, she wasn't really clear on much of anything. There were explosions, and running, and Nick needed someone to hold his hand to keep him from disappearing, and, oh, she'd just heard Mr. Friend's voice INSIDE OF HER HEAD before he'd been anywhere near her. The whole world felt as if it had tilted violently on its axis, and Cookie was falling, with no idea where or when she would land. Maybe she'd feel better if she just threw up?

But she kept it in and kept running until she, Nick, Jay, and the girl with the yellow eyes were deep in the woods behind the school.

"Wait . . . wait . . ." She heard Nick gasping for breath behind her. She stopped and turned around to see him leaning on a tree. Jay was still holding his hand and the girl with the yellow eyes (that were currently brown) stood nearby, clutching her backpack and smiling.

"Hi," she said. Her voice was a little raspy. Cookie stared at her eyes, which remained brown.

"Hey," Nick wheezed.

"Hello, my dear," Jay said, letting go of Nick's hand to give the girl a formal bow. Nick disappeared and then reappeared to the left of where he had been leaning on the tree, losing his balance and falling to the ground.

"Jay!" Cookie bleated.

"Sorry, sorry!" he yelped, jumping on top of Nick.

"You have to keep holding him! What if he rematerializes inside a tree?!?"

Nick blanched. "Oh my god, I hadn't thought of that," he whispered. "I could die."

Cookie glared at him. "And I'd be traumatized FOR LIFE."

Nick stood up quickly, dragging Jay with him. "YOU'D be traumatized? I'd be DEAD. This isn't about YOU."

Was this chubby nobody seriously yelling at Cookie Parker? She looked at him, her eyes narrowing with displeasure. Nick took one small step backward, and looked immediately smaller. Good. At least she still had some control over something, even if it was just Nick Gross.

"So," said the girl with the yellow eyes to Nick, "you can disappear?"

Cookie turned around to see that the girl's eyes were now a deep shade of violet. She felt her knees weaken. She'd been watching Nick disappear and reappear for the past twenty minutes, but there was something about this girl's eyes that was incredibly frightening.

"Say, that's neat," Jay said. "Do it again."

"Do what?" the girl asked.

"Your eyes," Nick said. "They just changed color." And at that the girl's eyes changed back to brown.

"Stop that," Cookie said.

"No, no no no," Jay said, his own eyes gleaming. "She shouldn't stop. She should never stop. This is AMAZING."

"I don't know if I can stop," the girl said. "I don't know what I'm doing." Her eyes changed to a leafy green.

"Whoa," Nick said.

"Did they just change?" the girl asked.

Cookie whipped out her cell phone. Already there were fourteen texts from Addison, Claire, and Izaak, but she ignored them and turned on her camera to snap a picture of the girl.

"Neat," the girl said when she saw the picture.

"My dear," Jay said, "this is EXTRAORDINARY." He turned to Nick. "You are also EXTRAORDINARY." Jay looked at Cookie.

"What?" she said.

"Have no doubt, you have always been extraordinary, Daniesha, but now you are even more so." Jay took a step toward Cookie while Nick stayed put, not-so-subtly trying to pull Jay back. "You, my dear, knew that Mr. Friend was going to come and get us before he was even out of the building." He lowered his voice. "You're clairvoyant."

"Shut up," Cookie snapped. "This isn't extraordinary, this is a nightmare." She looked at Nick. "What happens when this guy dematerializes in the middle of class? Or the exam? Or"—she pointed at the girl—"what happens when her eyes go all yellow again? The proctors are going to LOVE that."

"Oh, my delicious goddess who is sweeter than the baked good from which her nickname is derived, stop thinking so small. Exams. Please! Look at what is happening here!" Jay gestured wildly with both arms, inadvertently flapping Nick's. "Nick can transport himself! You can READ MINDS. This girl here—I'm sorry, my dear, what is your name?"

"I'm Martina."

"This lovely Martina can change her already beautiful appearance. And let's not forget that MR. FRIEND CAN CAUSE THINGS TO EXPLODE." Jay was jittery with excitement. "You have all become SUPERHEROES." He thought for a moment. "Except maybe Mr. Friend. He seemed maybe not so heroic. BUT STILL."

Cookie's head was pounding. She didn't know what was happening, but she knew that she wasn't feeling particularly heroic. "Shut up!" she said again. The noises in her head— *noises!* Not voices! She refused to believe that they were voices—were getting louder. "Shut up. Shut up shut up shut up shut up shutupshutupshutup." She sat down on a large rock and clasped her hands to her temples. This couldn't be happening. She was not going to be a freak. She was Cookie Parker, dammit, and she already had the power to make other people do what she wanted, so she might as well turn that power on herself and do what *she* wanted, and what she wanted was not to be a FREAK.

She felt a hand on her shoulder and looked up to see Martina kneeling next to her. Her eyes were dark gray. "Hi," the girl said again.

Cookie realized that tears were streaming down her cheeks, and she quickly wiped them off with the back of her muddy hand. "Are you going to tell me that everything is going to be all right?" she snapped at Martina.

"Oh, no," Martina said. "I was just saying hi. I have no idea how things are going to turn out."

JAY WAS THE FIRST TO SUGGEST THAT THEY FIND FARshad Rajavi. It made sense. With the exception of the driver, Jay explained, Farshad was the only person on the bus who they hadn't seen since the hospital, and Jay was eager to find out if he had a power, too. He was almost a little too excited about it, which was saying something, because Nick was used to Jay being extremely excited.

There had been some really weird days in Nick Gross's life. There was the day after his father's funeral, when he and his mother were finally alone in their house and had no idea what to do with themselves. They'd spent the entire day flopped on the couch, watching an impromptu movie marathon of random films (*The Lord of the Rings*, *They Live*, *Some Like It Hot*, *Ghostbusters*, and *Babe*) and eating fancy stuff from the gift baskets that people had sent, before finally getting up to order pizza. Then there was the first day back at school after the funeral where everyone except for Jay had acted like life was normal, which Nick supposed it was for them. But none were quite as strange as this day.

Cookie hadn't left her spot on the ground and didn't seem particularly inclined to move. Or talk. Nick was worried about her but had no idea what to do. It seemed to him that trying to make Cookie feel better would be like trying to make a caged lion feel better: *There, there, scary enormous cat that could murder and eat me, don't feel so glum.* Even Jay, who normally knew no boundaries, had the sense to leave Cookie alone. Nick knew that wasn't going to last. Distraction was key. "Maybe we should stay out of sight until we can maybe try to control our . . . powers?" Nick asked.

"RIGHT," Jay said. "Although I'm a little offended that you don't just want to hold my hand lovingly in yours forever." They both sneaked a look at Cookie. Not even an eye roll. Martina was scribbling something in her book. "Ah, well. Let's get started."

Teleporting was a strange experience. Nick never felt like he was disappearing and reappearing (what would that even feel like? Nick had no idea), but it was as if his vision jumped. One moment he'd be looking at Martina, and then Jay would let go of his hand and Martina would be a little bit more to the right than she had been. It was almost like looking at something up close and then winking one eye, and then the other. Nick never moved farther than a few inches, and he always moved to the left. After a while he could go for several minutes without teleporting. It seemed like progress.

"What if you aim to be somewhere?" Jay asked. "Try to want to be next to that stump."

Nick tried, but moved a few inches to the left, farther away from the stump.

"Huh," Jay said.

"Maybe he doesn't actually want to be near the stump," Cookie said. She had moved from her spot on the ground and was leaning against a tree.

"Now, why wouldn't he want to be closer to the stump?" Jay asked.

"Because it's a smelly, rotting old stump?"

"Interesting theory. Okay, Nick, let's try to visualize the stump as a place where you'd actually want to be."

Four inches to the left.

"I don't know how good Nick's imagination is," Martina observed. She was writing or drawing something in her sketchbook again. Cookie was now trying to take furtive peeks over the girl's shoulder without looking like she was interested.

Four inches to the left.

"You know what I'm noticing?" Jay said. "Nick isn't naked."

Four inches to the left.

"You noticed that, too? That was one of the first things I noticed about him," Cookie said sarcastically.

"Really?" Martina asked, looking up at Nick momentarily. "I hadn't really thought about it."

"He's teleporting with his clothes on," Jay explained. "When he jumps, his clothing jumps, too. Here," he said, picking up a rock and handing it to Nick, "see if this moves with you."

Nick held the rock in his hand. Four inches to the left. The rock was still in his hand.

"So this means that if he's holding on to something, he can teleport with it."

"Yay," Cookie said. "You won't be randomly showing up places butt nekkid."

"Well, that's a relief," Nick said. What a horrifying thought. Four inches to the left. The rock remained in his hand.

"Oh, Nick, the human body is a beautiful thing," Jay said. "If I lived in a warmer climate and didn't need pockets I would be unabashedly naked all the time."

Nick turned red, refusing to look at Cookie and Martina as Jay continued. "He can hold a rock and make it move, but he can't hold on to one of us and take us with him when he teleports. Here, hold his hand," he instructed Cookie, dragging Nick toward her.

"You hold his hand," she snapped.

"Very well." He grabbed Nick's hand. "Engage!"

"Excuse me?" Nick asked. Jay's hand was clammy and he was kind of tired of having to hold it.

"Go on, my good man, engage! Engage the teleportation device! Go! I'm ready!"

Nick squeezed his eyes shut and thought about moving. Nothing.

"Did it work?" Jay asked.

"Do you feel like you've moved at all?" Cookie rolled her eyes.

"Not particularly. Okay, Nick. Concentrate now. Go!" Nothing.

Martina chewed on her pen for a moment and then continued to draw.

Jay looked disappointed. "Shame. You can teleport your clothing and rocks, but not another person. Interesting interesting interesting. So even if you find yourself in a stressful situation, you won't move if someone is anchoring you. I think we're just about ready to go pay Farshad Rajavi a little visit."

Why do you draw yourself looking like an alien?

My sister calls me "Martian."

That doesn't mean you have to draw yourself like one.

FARSHAD HEARD THE FRONT DOORBELL RING, FOL-
lowed by his mother calling up to his room. "Farshad,
your friends are here to see you!"

If he were asked to come up with a wildly unbelievable statement, "Farshad, your friends are here to see you"
would be in stiff competition with "Farshad, there's a dolphin
growing out of your forehead" and "Racism is over!" He sat up
in his bed as Jay Carpenter, Nick Gross, Cookie Parker, and the
brown-haired girl from the bus filed into his room, followed
by his mother. Nick and the brown-haired girl were holding
hands. Farshad could not think of one thing to say.

"Farshad, they came to see how you are doing!" His mother
was entirely too excited about them being there, and Farshad
felt a twinge of guilt for not ever having any friends over. Not
that he could, seeing as how he didn't have any friends to in-
vite over, but he'd kind of been hoping that his mother hadn't
noticed that. Judging by her unadulterated glee at the sight
of the strange group, she'd definitely noticed. "Would you kids
like anything to drink or eat?" she asked them.

"No thank you," Nick and Cookie said in unison as Jay said,
"Why, yes, Dr. Rajavi, that sounds wonderful! Do you have any
delicacies from your native land?" The brown-haired girl just
smiled.

"We're FINE, thank you," Cookie said. She was clearly
on edge, which made sense, seeing as how she was in Far-

shad's terrorist-cell bedroom with some weirdos she normally wouldn't have given the time of day to.

"Thanks, Mom," Farshad said. "I think we just want to hang out. Is that right? Is that what we're doing here?"

"Yes, thank you," said Nick. He looked deeply uncomfortable, like Farshad himself. Sitting in bed while wearing Batman pajamas wasn't exactly the way he usually presented himself. The whole scene was bizarre. His mom backed out of the room, smiling like a lunatic.

"So," Farshad said, desperately trying to maintain some semblance of dignity, "hello, *friends*."

Nick cleared his throat. "Hey, man. How are you doing?"

"Well," Farshad said slowly, "I was in a major accident yesterday, so I'm a little achy. Also, four people who I hardly know just lied to my mother and told her that we're all good buddies, and now they're in my room looking at my stuff. How's it going with you?"

"We shouldn't have come here," Cookie grumbled. "He doesn't know anything."

"I know you think it's awesome to tell people that I'm an international terrorist. Am I wrong? I don't think I'm wrong." Farshad felt himself getting angry. "So why are you here? Come to blame me for the bus accident? Because it was all part of my evil terrorist scheme?"

The brown-haired girl put down his copy of *Persepolis* that

she had been thumbing through and looked up at Nick. "You shouldn't stress him out," she told Farshad.

Nick looked around the room. "I'm fine," he said, but that didn't stop Jay from grabbing hold of Nick's other arm. Cookie was also looking worriedly at Nick. No one spoke.

Jay cleared his throat. "Say, Farshad, old sport, you wouldn't happen to have any strange new superpowers now, would you?" He seemed perfectly serious. Normally, Farshad wouldn't take anything Jay Carpenter said seriously, because the kid was pretty much the school nutball, but Nick and Cookie were also looking at him as though Jay's question was valid. The brown-haired girl was looking at his soccer posters.

"No," Farshad said carefully, "not that I know of. You?"

"Farshad," Nick said, "we saw you. We were there on the bus. We saw what you did."

"What exactly did I do?"

"We saw you lift the bus seat off of Mr. Friend's leg."

That? That was nothing. Farshad might be avoiding team sports, but he still kept in shape. "Yeah," he said, "I exercise. Lots of people do. It's actually not a big deal."

Nick looked at him. "It's a big deal when the bus seat was bolted and welded to the floor."

Ridiculous. "The accident must have shaken it loose."

"From being bolted and welded to the floor?"

"Sure. Or something like that. It was an old bus. Is this why you came to see me today? To figure out how I lifted a seat? It's called 'staying fit.' Maybe you want to give it a shot one day." Farshad looked back down at his dad's laptop to the article about sinkholes that he'd been reading before they came in. *Get out. Get out. GET OUT.* "Bye, *friends.*"

Cookie turned to Jay with a worried look on her face. "You got him?"

Jay nodded. "Yes, m'lady." He was still holding Nick's arm.

Why was Cookie Parker of all people so worried about Nick? And why were they all being so touchy-feely?

Cookie glared at Jay, clearly displeased with the "m'lady" comment, and sat down on Farshad's bed. *Cookie. Parker. Is. Sitting. On. My. Bed. WHAT.*

"Look," she said, "I get that you're all pissed and stuff, but get over it, because freaky things are happening and you're part of it. I have spent the last hour with these weirdos and I've seen some strange stuff, so take your butt out of your head for a hot minute and listen to what we have to say, because we saw you. We saw you rip the seat out of the floor like it was nothing. That's not normal. Now we want to know if you've been able to do anything else not normal since the accident."

GET. OFF. OF. MY. BED. "I've pretty much been just sitting here all day. Did you suddenly gain the power to talk to people you think you're better than? Spooky."

Cookie turned back to Nick. "He's being a jerk," she said. "Just show him."

"I don't know . . . ," Nick said.

"He thinks we're insane, and I don't blame him, because we *sound* totally insane. Just show him already."

"Fine," Nick said, shaking Jay off his arm.

The brown-haired girl looked up at Farshad. "Don't worry," she said.

Jay took a step back and Nick took a deep breath.

And then he was gone. Sort of. He was still in the bedroom, but he'd moved a few inches without moving. Jay stepped up to him and grabbed his arm again.

As much as Farshad hated to agree with Cookie Parker about anything, she was right. That was not normal.

COOKIE HAD TO GIVE FARSHAD CREDIT FOR KEEP-
ing it together. She had been watching Nick teleport for about an hour and was still not used to it.

So much weird had happened in that hour. Cookie was having trouble wrapping her pounding brain around it. Nick's disappearances. Martina's eyes. Mr. Friend. And the voices . . . They'd been pretty quiet since they'd arrived at Farshad's house, just like they'd quieted down a bit in the woods when most of the students had dispersed.

It had become pretty clear that Nick only teleported when he was under stress. Maybe Cookie was the same way? The explosions and fire alarms had freaked her out and the voices had gotten louder, so maybe that was it. Maybe this would all go away. Maybe it would be okay and things would go back to normal and she'd never have to talk to these weirdos again. Cookie looked up. Everyone was still quiet.

It was a little unnerving to be in Terror Boy's bedroom, not just because he was potentially a terrorist (although, let's be honest, probably not), but mostly because Cookie had never been inside a bedroom before that belonged to a boy to whom she wasn't related. He had a lot of full bookshelves, more books piled on a desk, and a really nice rug that was half covered with dirty boy clothes. She did her best to avoid looking at a discarded pair of boxer briefs. Were they clean? Why wouldn't he put them in a hamper? *Boys are gross.*

Farshad stared at Nick. "That was different," he finally said. "Yeah," Nick said.

Farshad thought a moment. "And it explains why you ended up in the field instead of in the bus with the rest of us."

"Eureka!" Jay exclaimed. "I knew it was a good idea to bring you on board. Now," he continued, "do you think you're up to lifting something very heavy? Let's go outside and test your abilities on your mom's car."

"Jay, just give him a second," Nick said. "This is a lot for anyone to take in."

"Nonsense, my good man," Jay said. "He's a stalwart man, he can handle it." He turned to Farshad. "For the sake of propriety, we'll leave your room right now so that you can disrobe and put on something different. Not that I don't appreciate your superhero pajamas, but if you're going to be lifting a car, you might want to wear some dungarees or something. And once you're ready, we'll find Mr. Friend and combine powers to stop him from setting the entire town ablaze."

"Wait, what?" Cookie's mouth hung open a moment as she glared at Jay. "Is that what you think this is? That we're going to band together to become some sort of crazy explosive-substitute-teacher fighters?"

"Wait, crazy what now?" Farshad asked.

"Of course," Jay said. "Why else would you have been given these marvelous powers?"

Cookie's head swirled. She looked at Nick. "Is this what you think is happening?!?"

Nick shrugged. "I honestly don't know what to think. I'm just trying to figure out how not to get stuck in a wall without holding someone's hand."

Cookie looked at Martina, whose eyes had turned a deep blue. "Sure," she said.

"Sure, what?" Cookie asked.

"I'm in," Martina said.

"Excellent!" Jay exclaimed.

Cookie glowered at her. "And how exactly are you going to stop Mr. Friend?" she asked. "Attack him with a series of rapid eye-color changes?"

"Do you think that would work?" Martina asked. "It doesn't seem like the best strategy."

"You're weird," Cookie growled.

"Now, now, dearest chocolate-skinned empress of my heart," Jay began. "I realize that discovering your true destiny is a lot to take in—"

"This is CRAZY." Cookie stared at all of them: Nick, clearly nervous and hand in hand with Jay, who was jittery with excitement. Martina, now green-eyed and serenely unbothered by the heaping pile of madness that she'd just been dragged into (strangely enough, by Cookie herself). Farshad, the would-be terrorist in his messy bedroom wearing Batman pajamas. This was her destiny? These were her people? Never ever never. For her entire life—up until this point—every ounce of her formidable social powers had gone into preventing just such a fate. She was the only black girl in all of Muellersville and had somehow managed to climb her way to the top of the social order to become the most popular and powerful person in school, and she was not about to watch it all come crashing down around her. No. No. NO.

Cookie was trembling now with the effort it took not to scream. "We are not combining powers or banding together or forming the League of Incredible Nerds with Nearly Useless Powers," she said, painfully aware that she was sounding more hysterical with each word.

"Then why are you even here?" Nick asked coldly. "Why don't you just leave?"

Cookie was stunned. Nick Gross has just told *her* to leave. No one spoke. They all just stared at her.

"Fine," Cookie said, gathering her things. "I will."

Jay looked pained. "Daniesha . . ."

"Actually," Farshad said. "I think you should all leave."

FARSHAD WENT TO HIS WINDOW AND WATCHED AS they walked down the street and disappeared around the corner, Cookie marching angrily ten paces ahead of Nick, Jay, and Martina. Well, they didn't actually disappear, Farshad considered; he just couldn't see them anymore. If someone was around the corner, that person would probably be able to see them, so they didn't disappear. No, he knew now what disappearing really looked like.

He was having a hard time taking it all in. Strange powers? Nick could definitely teleport, and Martina's eyes had changed color, but it was unclear what Cookie could do (besides be a terrible human being, but that wasn't a sudden superpower so much as a nasty personality trait). Jay seemed to believe that the bus accident had given Nick the ability to disappear and reappear, and that the same accident had given Farshad some sort of strength. He looked at his hands. Was he really stronger than he had been before yesterday? He didn't feel particularly strong. Farshad sat down at his desk and picked up his pen. It snapped in half, spilling ink all over his desk blotter. He grabbed a pencil and began to write. It also snapped in half.

Weird.

Farshad gingerly picked up the pointy half of the pencil and made a list.

People on the bus during the accident

Nick

Cookie

Me

Mr. Friend

Martina

Bus Driver

Farshad looked over the names. Maybe he'd kicked them out of his room too soon. He kind of didn't know exactly why he'd done it, other than that he was uncomfortable and didn't like any of them and wanted to be alone. Farshad supposed that was reason enough.

He thought back to the accident. Lifting the bus seat had been surprisingly easy. Nick was probably right—those things were bolted and welded to the floor, so Farshad wouldn't have been able to lift it under normal circumstances. But there were many well-documented cases of women lifting and tossing entire cars to get to their babies who were pinned underneath. He had probably been energized by the trauma of it all and that had given him a brief shot of super strength. That had to be it (even though Farshad wasn't a mother and Mr. Friend was certainly not his baby).

He looked at the fresh ink stain on his desk. Only one way to tell.

Farshad changed into a T-shirt and a pair of jeans and went to the garage, where his mother's car was parked. Feeling a little silly, he squatted down next to the passenger side, grabbed hold of the bottom of the frame, and tried to lift it.

Nothing. Farshad let go of the car, sat down on the garage floor, and laughed at himself. Yes, something very strange was definitely going on with the others but he was perfectly—

The car hadn't moved, but there were two deep dents where Farshad's thumbs had been. It looked almost like that section of the car had been made out of tinfoil.

Not normal.

Farshad went into his backyard to find a rock, putting it in the palm of his hand and wrapping his fingers around it. He squeezed and opened his hand. The rock looked exactly the same. He put his thumb on it and pressed down. The rock cracked into a bunch of smaller pieces, as if it were made out of sugar.

Definitely not normal.

By the time Farshad felt ready to come back into the garage, he'd pulverized seven stones and ripped a small tree out of the ground using only his thumbs. He'd tried to do things without using his thumbs, but nothing particularly interesting had happened. Yet whenever he gripped anything with his thumbs or just applied pressure to something using his thumbs, he would destroy or seriously damage the thing he touched.

Farshad went back to his mother's car, hooked his thumbs under the bumper, and lifted. The whole back of the car rose an inch. He let it down gently and went back to his room and picked up a new pen, this time holding it in his fist like a toddler with a crayon.

> <u>People on the bus</u>
> <u>during the accident</u>
>
> Nick: teleportation
> Cookie: ?
> Me: thumb strength
> Mr. Friend: ?
> Martina: Can change eye color
> Bus Driver: ?

Someone was missing. He added one more line.

> Amish Kid?

Farshad heard his father's car pull up, so he slipped the list into his notebook. When he got downstairs his mother was preparing dinner and in a very good mood.

"Farshad had friends over today," she chirped to his father.

"Oh really?" Dr. Rajavi asked, and gave his son a surprised look.

God. Both of Farshad's parents knew that no one liked him. They'd probably been discussing his loserness with each other for ages.

"They wanted to make sure he was all right, isn't that nice?" His mom began chopping apricots for the chicken tagine. Chicken tagine was the sort of thing that she only cooked when she had the time, which was never. It was delicious. Farshad briefly considered getting into bus accidents and staying home from school more often.

"Very nice," his father said. "You should let them know that they can visit anytime."

"I made sure to tell them as they were leaving. Would they like to come over again soon?" his mother asked hopefully. "That Jay was very interested in my cooking."

"Sounds like he has excellent taste!" Farshad's father laughed and looked at him. "Well?"

"Well, what?"

"Are your friends going to be coming over again?"

Farshad watched his mother put the apricots into the slow cooker. When he was little he used to painstakingly sort all of the dried apricot bits out of the dish and save them until the end of the meal because he loved them so much. His mother still always made sure to put extra in. "Sure," Farshad said, "or maybe I'll hang out with them after school tomorrow."

His parents beamed, and Farshad wasn't sure whether he'd lied to them or not. He didn't have too much time to think about it before the front doorbell rang again.

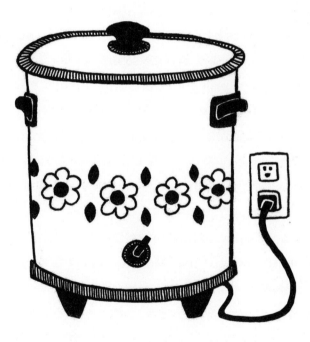

DON'T FOLLOW ME," COOKIE SAID AS THEY WALKED away from Farshad's house, as if Nick had actually been trying to follow her. (Jay might have been, but that was a different story.) "And don't try to contact me. None of this ever happened. I'm out." She quickly stomped off. Jay watched her go with a sigh.

"She is magnificent," he said.

"She seems angry," Martina said.

"Maybe she'll cool down soon," Nick said.

"I think she likes being angry," Martina said. She had a sort of almost absentminded way of saying things that shouldn't have been true but probably were. Nick found her a little unnerving. Then again, it was an unnerving sort of day.

"She's just passionate," Jay said with a dismissive wave of his hand, letting go of Nick. Nick blinked out of sight and reappeared a few inches to his left. Jay quickly grabbed Nick's arm again. "Are you okay?"

"Yeah, sure." They walked down the street for a minute, and Nick gradually realized that Martina was still with them. "We should probably get back to my house," Nick said. He looked at Martina. "Would you like to come with us?" he asked.

"Of course she would," Jay said, "she's with us now." Martina smiled, as if hanging out with Nick and Jay were some sort of prize.

They made it back to Nick's house without any more accidental teleporting. Nick could see his mother through the kitchen window, standing in front of the fridge, looking a little frantic. That probably meant that they were going to have takeout for dinner again. "Are you going to tell her?" Jay asked.

"I honestly hadn't thought about it," Nick admitted. "Do you think she'll freak out?"

Jay thought for a moment. "Angela is a strong and independent woman who has been through a lot. But she will absolutely freak out." He turned to Martina. "Will you tell your parents?"

"I don't tell them anything now," she said.

"You're mysterious." Jay sagely nodded his head. "That's definitely the superhero way."

What would Nick's mother say? What would she do? She'd probably take him to a doctor to find out what was wrong with him. Would he have to go to a hospital again? Probably. They'd probably hook him up to all sorts of machines and poke him with needles, because disappearing and reappearing was not in any way normal. Nick really didn't want to go back to the hospital. "Maybe I'll hold off on telling her for a bit until I have a better idea about what's going on," he said.

"Want me to stay over for dinner?" Jay asked.

"Yeah," Nick said. "Chinese or pizza?" He looked at Martina, who still wasn't going anywhere. "Would you like to stay for dinner as well?"

"Sure," she said.

"Do you have to call your parents?"

"No."

They went inside, and almost immediately Nick's mom grabbed both him and Jay and hugged them so violently that their heads smacked together. "I'm sorry!" she said, still holding them so tightly that Nick felt that his ribs might crack.

"Mom," Nick gasped, "it's nice to see you, too . . ."

"WHERE WERE YOU TWO?" she bellowed as she let go of the boys. "Do you have any idea what's been happening?" Nick's mother looked over to where Martina was quietly standing. "Hello?"

"Mom, this is our friend Martina—"

Mrs. Gross was already hugging Martina, who for the first time since Cookie had grabbed her in the field looked genuinely shocked.

"Do your parents know you're here?" Mrs. Gross asked.

Martina, whose eyes had turned a vibrant green, shook her head.

"Take this," Nick's mom said, putting her cell phone into Martina's hand. "Call your parents to let them know you're safe." She whirled around and looked at Jay. "You're next."

Martina was speaking quietly on the phone and it took Nick a moment to realize that he couldn't understand a word she was saying. His mom and Jay were also looking at her with fascination. "I think it's Russian," Jay whispered so that Martina wouldn't be distracted (even though his whispering was as loud as Nick's regular talking voice). Martina got off the phone and handed it to Jay.

"Spasiba!" he declared.

Martina giggled. *"Pozhaluysta."* Nick looked at her quizzically. "It means 'You're welcome,'" she explained as Jay left a message on his mother's voicemail.

"Hallo, Mother! It is I, your son, Jay Hieronymous Carpenter! I am at young Nicholas Gross's familial abode, where I will most likely be dining tonight!" He shot a look to Nick's mom, who rolled her eyes and nodded. "Good night!"

"Mom, why did they have to call their parents?" Nick asked.

Nick's mother ran her fingers through her hair, which seemed to have more and more gray strands in it every day. "Come, come look," she said, leading them down the short flight of stairs to the den. The television was on and the local news anchor was talking excitedly. "It's a special report," Nick's mom told them. "I was watching a cooking show . . ."

"You were going to cook something?" Nick asked.

"You be quiet. I was watching a cooking show and this"— she gestured to the anchorman—"started. That was an hour and a half ago. This has been going on for an hour and a half!"

She turned to Nick. "When you didn't come home immediately I was so scared. We're going to look into getting you a cell phone."

"Excellent. Can I have one, too?" Jay asked.

There was footage from a security camera of the school's parking lot, and Nick watched as a car exploded. The newscaster had clearly been replaying the footage over and over again.

Nick's mom turned to him. "There have been four car explosions so far. One by the school, one by the hospital, one next to the William Blake Mall, and another near the old bridge, and part of the forest near the school is on fire. Why didn't you two come straight home once the school was evacuated?"

"I'm sorry, Mom." Nick felt terrible. "We just thought it was a fire drill, and then we were sent home," he said, very quickly choosing to never, ever tell her that he'd witnessed two of the explosions firsthand. "Has anyone been hurt?"

"No, thank goodness, at least not as far as I know. Where *were* you?"

Nick found himself completely unprepared to answer her question with even a halfway decent lie. "Umm . . . walking around."

"Walking *around*?"

"I lost my backpack when we were evacuating," Martina

said. Sometimes it was strange to hear her speak. It was kind of easy to forget that she was there. Nick was dismayed to see that her eyes had turned a deep gray and desperately hoped that his mother wouldn't notice. "And then Jay and Nick were helping me find it."

"You know me!" Jay bleated. "Always there to help a damsel in distress."

"Yes, I know you." Nick's mom let out a deep breath and looked curiously at Martina, who smiled. "I'll get the take-out menu."

They sat down and watched the footage for the next hour until it became clear that the newscasters had nothing new to show. "I want you to stay inside," Nick's mom said as she shut off the television. Jay led Martina up to Nick's room. Nick trudged behind, frantically wondering how much dirty laundry was on his floor. He never much thought about the state of his room until some random girl was suddenly in it, which up to this point in his life had been NEVER.

"You should call Daniesha," Jay said as the door shut. "Mr. Friend is out there blowing up everything in his way, and according to the calculations I just made, he's probably looking for you."

"What makes you think that?"

"We're all looking for each other," Martina said. She sat

down on the floor, took out her sketchbook, and began to draw. She was very strange, but at least she didn't require a lot of attention or effort.

"Exactly," Jay said admiringly. "Everyone who was in the accident has been drawn to each other. You are linked."

"I'm pretty sure that's not true," Nick said, flopping down on his bed. "Besides, I don't have her phone number. Or a phone," he added lamely.

"We need to go out and find her," Jay said.

"Good luck getting out of this house," Nick countered. "Cookie is probably at home, just like us, safe and sound."

COOKIE HADN'T MADE IT TOO FAR BEFORE HER HEAD began to pound again. She sat down on a bench near the train station. The streets were oddly quiet for that time of day. At least there was that.

She looked at her phone. Izaak, Addison, Claire, and Emma were sending text after text about the car explosion, and the fire in the trees, and apparently there had been some more car explosions? It was difficult to decipher exactly what was going on from all the messages—Cookie's phone was buzzing non-stop. She felt a strong urge to shut it off entirely, but no, who did that? That would be crazy. She was a normal girl. She had friends. She was not crazy.

TURN RIGHT ON MAPLE! TWO BLOCKS, LEFT ON CE-DAR LANE!!! The words felt like they were splitting her head open, and less than a minute later she heard sirens. A fire truck with flashing lights came barreling around the corner. It went two blocks and then made the left onto Cedar Lane.

She looked at the street sign on the corner. MAPLE ROAD. Cookie took off running toward Cedar Lane.

Cookie saw the smoke before she turned the corner. Another car was on fire, and the firefighters were working to put it out. A policewoman approached her and asked if she lived on the block. Cookie said no.

"Go home," said the policewoman. "There's a lot of weird

stuff happening and it's better if everyone just stays inside their houses until we sort it all out, okay?"

Cookie turned and walked away, the smell of burnt rubber making her gag. Was it really that much safer inside? Houses seemed pretty flammable. She made it back to Maple and sat down on the side of the road, breathing deeply and willing herself not to throw up.

Cookie had known that the fire engine was coming because she had heard the driver figuring out the directions. Even if he'd been shouting them she shouldn't have been able to hear him from that far away and over the siren, so she had to have heard his thoughts, just like she'd heard Mr. Friend trying to get out of the school.

What other thoughts would she be able to hear? For a moment Cookie wondered if she could find out what Izaak really thought about Addison, and then shuddered at the idea. Her stepsister had once warned her never to look in her step-brother's room, because teenage boys were all disgusting and the less you knew about them the better. Cookie wasn't particularly close with her stepsiblings (they were much older and both in college), but that had always seemed like sound advice.

What if she could read her mother's mind? Or her stepfather's? Cookie had never given too much thought to what her mother and George were thinking, and didn't particularly feel like starting now. What if she heard something terrible that she'd never be able to unhear? Cookie began to wonder if she would ever be able to go home again.

No. NO. This wasn't right. She was Cookie Parker and she wasn't supposed to be afraid of anything. Yet there she was, paralyzed, without any idea of what to do next. *Get a grip, Cookie*, she told herself and took a deep breath. She had to figure out what she was going to do before her mother started calling.

They had always been close. Around the time that Cookie's mom had been about to graduate from college, she became pregnant. Carmen Parker had refused to marry Cookie's biological father, even though he'd made the offer. She had turned him down because she was not going to get married to anyone out of obligation. After graduation, Cookie's biological father had moved to California, and every year he sent her a stuffed animal on her birthday. Sometimes she wondered if she'd still be getting stuffed animals when she was in college.

Cookie's mother decided to go it alone, and named her only daughter after her brother—Cookie's uncle Danny—who had died in Iraq, and up until Cookie was five, it had been just the two of them. Carmen would go to work and take Cookie to the day care at her office. Cookie remembered her mother sneaking in to see her in the middle of the day. But Carmen didn't like the elementary school in their Philly neighborhood, so she took an accounting job in Muellersville.

The family they left behind in Philadelphia thought they were crazy for moving. "Why in the world are you moving all the way out there?" Cookie remembered her grandmother asking. "There's nothing out there but cows and Amish people." She hadn't been wrong. Muellersville was surrounded by farms with silos and barns and cows and cows and cows. A lot of the kids at school whose parents didn't work for Auxano lived on those farms, and Cookie had heard stories of those kids getting up at 4:30 every morning to do farm stuff. Cookie was never completely sure what "farm stuff" was (because, like she'd ever talk to the farm kids . . . *please*) but getting up at 4:30 A.M. was pretty unthinkable, so she got where her grandmother was coming from.

But her mother had insisted. The schools were better, the homes were cheaper, and Auxano was offering her a steady job with a good salary, so they moved away from their family and other black people, and everyone and everything familiar. After a few years, Cookie's mom had met George MacKessy, and the next thing Cookie knew it wasn't just the two of them anymore.

Not that there was anything wrong with her stepdad. He was fine. Super nice to Cookie's mom, and his two grown kids,

London and Dallas (his ex-wife must have really liked place names), were decent and welcoming. But Cookie had been used to having her mother all to herself, and all of a sudden George was around all the time, and even if he wasn't around, her mom told him everything that Cookie told her, so it was like he was around all the time anyway. Cookie used to tell her mom everything, but that hadn't happened in a long while.

Cookie had no plans to tell her mother about Nick's and Martina's new . . . abilities. The others hadn't really discussed it, but the way that they'd all kind of wordlessly agreed to sneak around made it pretty clear that, at least for now, they were keeping it between just them. Oh, and Farshad. And *Jay*. Ugh.

The Shrimp, his best friend, Terror Boy, and . . . Weird Girl. She definitely needed a better nickname. If ever there was a club that Cookie did not want to be a part of, there it was. And yet, as she sat there, Cookie realized that all she wanted to do was find them and tell them what she'd heard and seen. *Pathetic.*

FARSHAD COULD HEAR A MAN'S VOICE TALKING frantically to his mother, and it didn't sound pleasant.

"You don't understand, Mrs. Rajavi, I need to speak to your son."

"That's Dr. Rajavi," Farshad heard his mother say. He smiled. His mother had worked very hard to earn her doctorate, and she never let anyone forget it.

"Mr. Rajavi—" The voice was getting louder. It sounded familiar.

"I am also Dr. Rajavi," Farshad's father said. His parents loved this routine. *Dr. Rajavi? Which Dr. Rajavi? We are both Dr. Rajavi! Do you mean the Dr. Rajavi that can cook well? We can both cook well! The Dr. Rajavi who is very attractive? Why, we're both very attractive! The Dr. Rajavi who enjoys musical theater? That's both of us, too! This is so confusing! How will we ever figure out to whom you intend to speak?* They'd been doing it for years, and Farshad suspected that people were only amused by it because jolly brown people with weird accents are funny.

The voice didn't seem amused. "Dr. Rajavi, it is imperative that I speak to your son right now!" The familiar voice was shaky and pleading. Farshad popped his head through the hallway door to see who it was.

Mr. Friend was standing at the front door. He was wearing a full-length coat and looked sweaty and unshaven. Farshad felt afraid.

"Farshad Rajavi!" the man yelled. Farshad's mom moved instinctively in front of Farshad. "I have to talk to you. I have to. I've been looking for you all day. Please listen to me."

"What is this about?" Farshad's mother looked at Farshad.

"I have no idea," Farshad said. But from what Nick and the others had told him, Mr. Friend was dangerous. The fires. The explosions he had seen on television. He had to get Mr. Friend out of the house. "Maybe I should just go and talk to him."

"Excuse me?" his mother asked him in rapid-fire Farsi. *"You are going nowhere with this dirty, crazy man."*

"Sir," Farshad's father said, "our son has been through a traumatic accident and needs his rest. You should go."

"I know!" Mr. Friend shouted. "I know! I was in the accident, too! I need to talk to him! Farshad—"

"Go to your room right now!" his mother ordered, and Farshad obliged, slowly making his way up the stairs.

"No. NO. YOU DON'T UNDERSTAND. HE'S IN TERRIBLE DANGER. WE'RE ALL IN TERRIBLE DANGER—"

"SIR!" Farshad's father bellowed. "You are becoming unhinged! Please leave my house!"

"I will call police officers!" his mother yelled.

"PLEASE. NO, YOU DON'T UNDERSTAND. IT'S HAPPENING AGAIN. YOUR SON IS IN DANGER—"

Farshad heard a popping sound, and suddenly his mother was screaming. He rushed to the kitchen to see his parents using dish towels to furiously beat out a small fire that had started on the counter—it looked as though his mother's slow cooker had exploded. Chickpeas and bits of apricots were everywhere.

"Lock up the house!" his father yelled, and before Farshad shut the front door, he saw Mr. Friend limping down the street, his long overcoat opened to reveal that he was still wearing a hospital gown.

The Drs. Rajavi quickly put out the fire and called the police. Farshad went back to his room and reopened his father's laptop, taking great care not to use his thumbs.

NICK STARED AT THE EMAIL FOR A MINUTE BEFORE showing it to Jay and Martina.

From: frajavi@deborahread.edu
To: ngross@deborahread.edu

Mr. Friend was just at my house and is clearly disturbed. I don't think we're safe. Can we meet?

Farshad

Nick had spoken with Farshad twice in the past twenty-four hours, and both times the guy had been pretty rude. Why would he want to help them now? What had happened?

"That's a short email," Jay observed, getting excited. "Do you think he was writing it under duress? Maybe Mr. Friend was standing over him, dictating what to write. Maybe it's a trap!"

Nick frowned. "Why would Mr. Friend tell him to write that he was 'clearly disturbed'? That makes no sense."

"If it were a trap, he probably would have had to write something like 'I have ice cream. Come over for ice cream,'" Martina chimed in, still sketching in her book.

"That would be kind of random," Nick said.

"Do you like ice cream?"

"Sure. Who doesn't like ice cream?"

"Exactly."

"Good thinking, everyone," Jay said, pacing the short length of Nick's bedroom. "I think you should go see Farshad."

Nick looked at him. "Who, me?"

"Well, you're the only one who can go," Jay said.

"Like my mom is going to let me out of the house." Nick ran his fingers through his hair. Martina quickly reached up and grabbed his arm to prevent him from teleporting. "I'm okay," he said. She shrugged and let go.

"The lovely Angela won't even notice that you're gone," Jay said.

"Of course," Nick said, throwing up his hands. "And how am I supposed to get out of the house without my mom noticing?"

Jay put his hand on the wall next to Nick's desk. "How thick do you think these walls are?"

Nick stared at him. "You can't be serious."

Jay knocked lightly on the wall. "It's probably thicker than four inches. Probably."

Martina also knocked on the wall. "Probably," she said.

"Oh, you can tell that from knocking?" Nick was getting agitated. Jay grabbed his hand.

Martina furrowed her brow. "Also, he'd end up fifteen feet in the air."

"Bad plan," Jay said, turning back to Nick. "You'd better just sneak out through the back door, into the garage, and go out from there."

"My mother will definitely notice the garage door opening," Nick said.

Jay looked him straight in the eye. "Then don't open the garage door."

Lately, before making any big decisions, Nick had started wondering what his dad would have done. Before he got sick, his dad had worked in Auxano's IT department, but spent a lot of his time volunteering at a local food pantry. Nick's mom was always talking about how he'd really liked working "with the good guys," so Nick would try to think of what a guy who liked working with good guys would do. It wasn't easy. Nick's father had been in and out of the hospital since Nick was six, so he didn't remember him as a person who worked with good guys.

But Nick remembered that he loved his dad, and that his dad had loved him. He remembered the days spent in the hospital when they'd play cards together or watch movies or when his dad had tried to tell him stories about his life, like when he first kissed a girl in high school or how he took a year off from college to backpack around the world. His dad had known that he probably wouldn't be around to tell them to Nick when Nick'd be old enough to actually understand what his dad was saying.

Of course, Nick's dad had never told him any stories about

what it was like to suddenly find out that you have supernatural abilities. Nick wished he knew what his dad would have thought of the whole situation, and wishing it made him feel hollow inside. He looked at Jay and Martina and then left the room.

A moment later he was standing in the darkened garage between his mother's car and the closed garage door. He moved himself as close to the door as possible without his left arm touching it. And then he was outside. Nick began to run.

I just teleported through a solid door. I JUST TELEPORTED THROUGH A SOLID DOOR. Nick kept running and trying not to think about it. After a while he could only think about the stitch in his side. If he was going to have to keep running from explosions and running to save people, he was really going to have to get into better shape. Maybe eat a salad or something.

Nick staggered to a tree and leaned against it. He was about a block from Farshad's house, and the streets were very quiet except for his wheezing and the sound of footsteps behind him. Nick turned to see Cookie Parker.

"I heard you coming," she said, slowly lifting her hand and tapping her index finger to her temple. Her eyes were filled with tears.

Nick wiped the sweat off his forehead. He remembered what his father used to tell him, and how it would make him feel a little better even when he knew that it couldn't possibly be true: "It's going to be okay," Nick told her.

COOKIE AND NICK WOUND THEIR WAY SILENTLY back to Farshad's house. She didn't want Nick to see her all cry-faced again and it seemed like he didn't particularly want to see that, either.

A police cruiser was parked outside of the Rajavis' house. Nick ducked behind a tree. "What are you doing?" Cookie asked.

"The police are here!"

Cookie eyed Nick. "Are you a criminal?"

"No."

"Then why are you hiding?"

Nick looked sheepish. "My mom doesn't know I left the house."

Cookie rolled her eyes. "I genuinely don't believe that the police are going to call your mom." She looked worried. "I wonder why they're here."

"We need to find a way to let Farshad know that we're outside."

"You didn't email him back to let him know you were coming?" Nick had told Cookie about Farshad's email on the way there.

Nick looked flustered. "No, I just left. Can you use your phone to call him or email him?"

Cookie looked down at her phone. There were dozens of unread texts and two missed calls from her mom. She wasn't going to be able to avoid everyone for much longer, and it was almost evening. "I don't know if this is a good idea. He kicked us out of his house."

"He emailed me. He's trying to watch out for us." Nick took a deep breath. "Whether we like it or not, I think that we all need to start watching out for each other." He faced her. He was sweaty and kind of a mess. He held out his hand for her phone. She looked up at the Rajavis' house and saw Farshad looking down at them. He looked aggravated. Great.

"He's looking at us," Cookie told Nick, who whirled around and started waving at Farshad like a great big goober. Farshad gestured for them to meet him in the backyard.

"Why are the police here?" Cookie asked as soon as Farshad came out the back door. Farshad ignored her and looked at Nick. "Why are you out of breath?"

Nick looked pained. "Your email sounded urgent. I ran all the way here."

"Couldn't you have just . . . teleported here?" Farshad asked, annoyed.

"No," Cookie said quickly, "he can only go a couple of inches." She didn't know why, but she felt the need to defend Nick.

"I think it's about four," Nick said, wiping his brow. "Four inches at a time."

"And only to the left," Cookie added.

"Why did you bring her?" Farshad asked, shooting a look at Cookie.

Cookie was used to people giving her strange looks; it was par for the course in Muellersville for one of the town's two resident black people (the other one being Cookie's mother). She'd lived in the small town for seven years, but she still felt the stares when she went into nice stores with Addison and Claire. People who didn't know her were very careful when they talked to her, and sometimes even people who did know her were careful about what they said when she was around, as if they were afraid they'd offend her. Sometimes Cookie felt like she had a power over people like that. If they were going to be obviously nervous around her then she might as well take advantage of their fear. Ridiculous people.

But Farshad wasn't like that. He wasn't afraid of her; certainly he must have received his fair share of stares in Muellersville even before he became Terror Boy. He was the Arab Kid, just like Cookie was the Black Girl and Harshita Singh was the Indian Girl and Danny Valdez was the Hispanic Guy and Emma Lee was the Asian Chick. They should have all formed a posse long ago and walked around Muellersville together, just to freak people out. But Farshad seemed to hate her and had made sure that she was aware of his feelings. She didn't really understand what she'd ever done to earn that hate, but whatever. People had the right not to like each other. If he wanted to be a jerk to her, fine. Two could play that game. But like Nick had said, they needed to start watching out for one another. It was one thing to be a brown person in Muellersville and another to be a brown person in Muellersville with superpowers.

Or okayish powers, at any rate. Like it or not, they were stuck with each other.

"He didn't bring me. I heard him and I came," Cookie said.

Farshad looked at her and raised his eyebrows

"Why did you email Nick?" she asked him.

Farshad turned to Nick and began to recount his story. Cookie gasped when he told them about the exploding slow cooker, and he looked annoyed. "It's fine," he said, "we can buy another slow cooker."

"Did you see Mr. Friend do it?" Nick asked. "You know . . . explode the slow cooker?"

Farshad looked down at his hands. "Not exactly," he admitted. "But he was there. Then the slow cooker exploded. We've never had that happen before . . ."

"But what did he want from you?" Cookie interrupted.

"How should I know?" Farshad snapped.

"Do you think he knows what happened to us?" Nick asked.

"Well, whatever has happened to us, it looks like it's happened to him, too," Farshad said.

"Wait." Cookie looked at Farshad. "Are you admitting that something happened to you?"

"Cookie . . . ," Nick started.

"What? He calls us over here because all of a sudden he's so worried about us?"

"I didn't call *you*," Farshad said.

"Before, he didn't think that there was anything wrong with him and he couldn't have cared less about anything that we said. But now all of a sudden he's all worried." Cookie turned to Farshad. "We know Nick can teleport. Extremely short distances. And we know that I can read minds—"

"Actually, I didn't know that," Farshad said.

"Well, now you do. I can read minds, and you probably have super strength. Well?"

Farshad looked at her strangely. "You can read minds?"

"Sure," she said, sounding infinitely more confident than she actually felt about her newfound ability.

"Then what am I thinking right now?"

"Guys . . . ," Nick said.

"You're thinking that you hate me but you're too scared to say it so you choose to give me nasty looks instead," Cookie snapped.

Farshad let out a short, harsh laugh. "No," he said, "I was thinking of the number seven."

"Liar."

"Guys . . ."

"Faker."

"Guys . . ."

"Well, where's the super strength?" Cookie asked, ignoring Nick's weak attempts to calm them down. She'd had a rough twenty-four hours, and letting loose on creepy Terror Boy was actually making her feel more like her old self again: Strong. Sharp. Not afraid all the time.

Farshad looked around angrily, and found a large pebble. He squatted and put it on the flagstone patio, and lowered his thumb onto it.

The pebble shattered to dust.

"Whoa," Nick said.

Well, Cookie thought, *hello again, fear.*

FARSHAD HAD SCARED COOKIE. HE KNEW THAT, AND it gave him more pleasure than he cared to admit. He had to stop that sort of thinking—not just because his parents were good people who had strived to teach him the value of kindness, but because Cookie might read his thoughts.

The truth was, he had been thinking about the number seven, but he'd probably also been hating Cookie because, well, he'd always hated Cookie Parker. But he had to be careful. If she was telling the truth, then she could do a lot more damage than reducing some small stones to dust. Given the choice, he would have much rather had the power to read minds. That way he could be sure about what people really thought about him. Plus, it would probably help with academics.

"So Jay was right," Nick said. "You do have super strength."

"Sort of." Farshad looked down at his hands again, which yesterday had seemed perfectly normal and not particularly worthy of consideration. "It's really just my thumbs," he admitted.

"Wait," Cookie said, regaining her composure. "You have super-strong . . . thumbs?"

"Yeah, but didn't you already know that from reading my mind?"

Cookie sucked in a breath. "That's not how it works," she said.

"So how does it work?" Farshad asked.

"I don't exactly know," Cookie said. She looked at Nick, who shrugged.

"I don't know how any of our powers work," Nick said. "I can barely control mine. Martina is back at my house and her eyes are changing colors every two minutes. I think my mother might have noticed." He turned to Farshad. "Did you tell your parents about . . . this?" he asked, gesturing to the small pile of crumbled stone at their feet.

"No," Farshad said, looking back at his house.

"I didn't tell my mom, either," Nick said.

They looked at Cookie.

"I'm not telling anyone anything," she said. "Like we want to be connected to Mr. Friend in any way."

Farshad nodded. He hated agreeing with her, but the last thing that a guy whose nickname was Terror Boy needed was to have people know that he had super strength. Even his parents. Especially his parents. They already worried about him too much. He could see them through the kitchen window, cleaning the charred area where the destroyed slow cooker had been. "I'd better go back inside," he said.

"Wait," Cookie said.

"Do you think we should maybe get together soon?" Nick asked. "Like, all four of us? Talk all this over?"

"Wait," Cookie said.

"I don't know," Farshad said. "We should probably wait until this whole Mr. Friend business dies down."

"Wait," Cookie said.

"The police are probably going to catch up with him soon," Nick said. "I mean, if the guy is limping around in a hospital gown—"

"HE'S HEADING TO YOUR HOUSE." Cookie was staring straight at Nick. He stared back at her, the color draining from his face.

"My mom," he whispered, blinking out of existence and re-appearing four inches to the left of where he had just been.

Cookie grabbed his hand. "Let's go," she said, and turned to Farshad. "You coming?"

THEY WERE ALL RUNNING TOGETHER. COOKIE WAS keeping up but it was pretty apparent that Farshad could easily outrun them both. He wasn't even breathing hard. He was probably one of those guys who ran around for fun. Nick felt like his lungs were going to explode.

He was frantically worried. If Mr. Friend could blow up cars, and trees, and slow cookers, his mom was in danger. (What was a slow cooker, anyway? Nick had been sort of afraid to ask. He made a quick mental note to do an Internet search later, if his whole house wasn't on fire.) But Jay and Martina were also in his house. What would Mr. Friend do to them? What *could* he do? And what could they do to stop him?

Farshad stopped at the end of a block. "Where do you live again?" he asked Nick. He wasn't even sweating. Nick wheezed out his address and Farshad took off again.

"Stop," Cookie said. Nick stopped and looked at her but Farshad kept going. "STOP!" she yelled.

Farshad turned around and jogged back to them. "I was under the impression that we were in a hurry," he said.

"No . . . ," Cookie started.

"So you're not so certain that Mr. Friend is going to Nick's house?"

"I'm sure, I'm sure, I heard him," she said frantically to Farshad. "But now I'm hearing you."

Farshad frowned. "What am I thinking right now?"

"No, I can't hear you now."

"But you just said—"

"I just heard you figuring out how to get to Nick's house." Cookie looked at him, hard. "Is that what you were thinking?"

Farshad blanched, and was quiet.

"Yes," Cookie answered for him.

"What's going on?" Nick asked.

"Tell him," Farshad said.

"I just heard him again," Cookie whispered.

"What did he . . . think?"

"He was wondering about the best way to get to the library from here," Cookie said.

"Yes," Farshad said. "Can you hear what I'm thinking now?"

Cookie shook her head.

"Interesting," Farshad said. "How about now?"

"No."

"And now?"

"Eww! Stop that."

Farshad laughed.

"Come on, guys!" Nick said. The longer they stood there, the more chance there was that he would return to find his house engulfed in flames. His mom, his best friend, the weird but friendly girl that they were now apparently hanging out with, and everything his dad had ever owned would be gone. Nick looked at Farshad.

"She can hear thoughts," Farshad explained, "but only if someone is thinking about how to get somewhere. That's why she heard me but not you. You know how to get to your house—I had to figure it out."

"Oh, so that's why you could hear Mr. Friend trying to get out of the school," Nick said. "And him trying to find my house."

"Right!" Cookie said. "He is almost there. I can hear it."

"WE HAVE TO GO!" Nick yelled, and took off in the direction of his house. Farshad quickly caught up and jogged beside him.

Nick was trying to keep pace, but he had to know. "What were you thinking that grossed Cookie out?"

Farshad smiled. "Directions to the boys' bathroom at school."

COOKIE WAS TRYING VERY HARD NOT TO THINK about urinals, but Farshad had put the image in her head and she hated it. As they ran, he transmitted a few thoughts to her: *Turn left at the corner. Four more blocks, over the train tracks. Turn right.* She wondered if he was trying to annoy her. If he was, it was working.

She slowed down to let Nick catch up with her. "Do we have a plan?" she asked him.

"Save . . . my mom . . ." He looked miserable and sweaty.

"I'm sure your dad will be there to protect her if Mr. Friend shows up," Cookie said. Nick started running faster and she picked up her pace to keep up. What were they going to do to Mr. Friend? Tackle him? Cookie stopped running, took out her phone, and called 911. Farshad and Nick stopped.

"Is now really the time to make calls?" Nick asked.

"There's a crazy man outside threatening us and we're really afraid!" she told the emergency dispatcher, giving the address that Mr. Friend had unwittingly transmitted to her brain. "He's only wearing a jacket and a hospital gown!"

"Why didn't I think of that?" she heard Farshad mutter. *Because I'm smart,* she thought. *In control. Solving all the world's problems, one phone call at a time.* They started running again, and a police cruiser followed by a screaming fire engine passed them as they rounded the corner onto Nick's block.

Mr. Friend was in front of Nick's house, just as she knew he would be, and smoke was billowing out of two of the windows on the second floor. Farshad stopped abruptly and put out his arm to stop Cookie. "Oh god," she gasped as the firemen scrambled to hook up their gear. She looked to Nick, but he was gone.

"Where is he?" She looked around frantically and grasped Farshad's arm. "Where did he go?"

"Nick!" Farshad yelled. "NICK!" He turned to Cookie. "Can you hear him?"

"No!" she said, and realized he was asking if she could hear Nick's thoughts. She closed her eyes. Nothing. She opened them to see Mr. Friend running toward them. His face was streaked with soot and tears.

"RUN!" he screamed at them. "They're coming! RUN AND HIDE!!!"

Cookie screamed and Farshad stepped in front of her, holding his thumbs up in front of him. Mr. Friend stopped and looked at him quizzically. The three stood for a moment, staring at one another, until a horse appeared out of nowhere, galloping at them with what seemed like incredible speed. Cookie grabbed Farshad and pulled them both out of the way as a man jumped off the horse and tackled Mr. Friend to the ground.

AS HE FELL, A NEARBY TREE ERUPTED IN FLAMES, AND Cookie took off down the street with Farshad at her heels. They ducked behind a house a few down from Nick's house. Farshad began climbing the fence in the backyard.

"What was that?!?" Cookie yelled over the sounds of the sirens.

"I have no idea!" Farshad yelled back, his heart pounding in his ears as he bolted through someone's backyard.

"Where are we going?" Cookie yelled over the fence.

"Back to the house!"

"The house that's on fire?" she asked incredulously as she jammed herself through a crack in the fence.

"We have to help Nick," Farshad said, lithely jumping over another fence. She followed him, dodging someone's patio furniture.

"How?" she asked, scrambling over another fence and landing in a pile of wet leaves on the other side. Her mother was going to kill her when she saw her clothes.

Farshad whirled around. "With these," he said, holding out his thumbs again.

Cookie stared at him. "You're going to stop a fire with your thumbs?" she asked. In her mind she saw the hallways of her school, and the door to the boys' bathroom again. "STOP THAT."

Farshad snickered and she resolved to find a way to block

out his urinal thoughts and wipe that stupid smile off his face. She followed him over the last fence into Nick's backyard, where Martina and Jay stood, staring at the smoke billowing out of the second-floor windows. Tears were pouring down Jay's face and Martina was holding on to him. "I have to go in!!!" he was screaming. She was keeping him from running into the house.

"Shh shh shh," Martina said, still holding tight to Jay. She looked at Cookie. "Nick's mom ran back into the house to find him and we couldn't stop her."

Jay looked up at her and Farshad, his devastated face darting back and forth between them. "Where's Nick?"

HE'D HEARD HIS MOTHER SCREAMING HIS NAME, and the next thing he knew his lungs were filling with smoke and he couldn't see. He began to cough.

"NICK?" his mom managed to yell through her own coughing. He saw her stumbling through the smoke and grabbed her arms. He had her. He had to get her out.

He had no memory of getting in. Had he teleported that far? From the side of the road into a burning house? If he had been able to teleport in, he could teleport out. "Don't worry, Mom, I've got you," he wheezed, and concentrated as hard as he could on his front sidewalk. Soon they'd be safe.

"Sweetie, we have to get out!" his mother gasped, tugging at his arm. They hadn't moved. He couldn't use his power to save her. Nick began to feel dizzy.

He felt someone's hand on his back, shoving him through the smoke. Nick grabbed his mother and together they stumbled through the house toward the back door. It was only after firefighters with masks began to pour into the house that the pressure on Nick's back let up.

There was no one behind him.

The firefighters helped them to get out into the relief of the fresh air, where Nick doubled over and threw up on his mom's decorative garden gnome. He hadn't yet wiped his mouth when he was tackled by a sobbing Jay.

"I'm sorry!" Jay wailed as the paramedics extricated Nick from his embrace. They strapped Nick to a gurney and put an oxygen mask on his face, but in moments Jay was back at Nick's side. Nick smiled through his mask. Four burly first responders couldn't contain Jay Carpenter. Who really had the superpowers? He reached out his hand to comfort his friend.

Jay grasped it. "Don't worry, I got you," he whispered into Nick's ear. "I'm so sorry, Nick, old man." Jay's voice caught and he began crying again. "I tried to tell her that you weren't in there and I couldn't stop her, and I heard her screaming your name and I'M SO SORRY, NICK, I'M SO SO SO SORRY . . ."

Nick looked over to where his mother was lying on a gurney. She had been in the house longer than him and didn't look well. But she wasn't burned. Could someone still die of smoke inhalation if they got out in time? Nick's eyes brimmed with tears. He shouldn't have sneaked out of the house. Then his mom wouldn't have run back in looking for him.

"It's going to be okay," Nick said. His father's words again. He sat up and looked at his house. Firefighters were walking in and out, so it probably wasn't still on fire. He wondered how many of his dad's things had been damaged. His mom was going to be a mess. Nick looked to Farshad and beckoned him over. Cookie came, too.

"Where's Mr. Friend?" Nick asked in a low voice as soon as they were close.

"We don't know," Farshad said worriedly. "Someone . . . grabbed him."

"What do you mean, 'grabbed him'?" Nick asked. "How? Who?"

Cookie leaned in. "I think it might have been the Amish kid from the crash." She whispered, "He was on a horse."

Nick looked at Farshad, who nodded. "It came right at us, and the guy just jumped off and tackled Mr. Friend and we ran."

Jay looked at Cookie, his eyes red and puffy from crying. "Thank god you're okay," he said, throwing his arms around her. Cookie's eyes widened in shock and her body went completely stiff.

"What. Is. Happening," she said.

Farshad, who had been looking pretty grim, stifled a smile.

A pretty, young paramedic with freckles and red hair came and shooed them away, explaining that they were taking Nick and his mother to the hospital to make certain that they were all right. Jay ignored her and climbed into the back of the ambulance with Nick. "Are you family?" the paramedic asked.

"Yes," Jay said. She eyed him and Nick. "I am," Jay insisted, "and if you don't let me go to the hospital with my brother, I will run alongside the ambulance the entire way, screaming like a banshee. No one wants that."

The paramedic stared at him, seemed to do a quick mental calculation of the value of fighting him, and shrugged her shoulders. Five minutes later they were on the road, Jay uncharacteristically silent.

"How bad do you think the house was?" Nick asked him.

"I think it was probably mostly just smoke damage," Jay said. "We couldn't even tell where the fire started."

"So what happened?"

Jay closed his eyes. "The doorbell rang and then Martina—who, by the way, is really stellar; I don't know why we haven't been friends for years—and I heard Angela talking to someone. Mr. Friend. He sounded very put out. And then your smoke alarms went off, the house started filling with smoke, and we ran out." He swallowed hard. "And when your mom saw that you weren't with us, she ran back in. We tried to tell her that you weren't inside but she wouldn't listen. I couldn't stop her." He started to cry again. "Thank god you showed up in time and were able to find her. I wish I'd had the courage to run into a burning building."

Nick glanced at the paramedic, who was looking out the back window. "Actually," he said in a low voice, "I didn't run in."

Jay looked confused "You walked in?"

"No."

"You waltzed in?"

"No."

"You moseyed in?"

"No."

"Rode a horse in."

"Definitely not."

"Boogied in."

"When have I ever boogied anywhere? Think for a moment about how I might have gotten into the house."

Jay thought for a moment. "No."

"Yes."

"You didn't."

"I did."

"Did you mean to?"

"No."

Jay straightened up, his eyes twinkling, and he looked like his old self again. "Still, old man, this is a phenomenal development. Now that you know it's possible, you can do it again. Hopefully without the imminent destruction of your home and family as an impetus." He grinned. "We have so much work to do!"

Nick closed his eyes. His head was throbbing. "Can we not think about it right now?"

Jay stopped smiling. "But we must."

"Now?"

"Well," Jay said delicately, "where's Mr. Friend?"

AFTER THE AMBULANCE DROVE OFF, FARSHAD, Cookie, and Martina walked back to the road, none of them saying a word. Farshad felt both exhausted and wired, and he knew he would never get to sleep that night even if he tried. He really didn't want to think about going to bed, because that would mean going home and explaining to his parents why he disappeared, and lying to them again . . . Eventually, he was going to have to face them. But not yet.

"Okay," Cookie said, looking up from her phone.

"Okay, what?" Farshad asked.

"You were figuring out how to get to the hospital from here. I am not ready to go home, so let's all go. Okay?" she said, setting off in the direction of the hospital.

Farshad looked at Martina, whose eyes were brown again.

"Sure," she said, and set off after Cookie. Farshad sighed and followed.

They took the long way, sticking to the side streets. No one talked much. Cookie wasn't looking at Farshad, but as they walked he noticed her jaw tensing up every time he tried to figure out which street to take. Martina walked calmly alongside them, as if their worlds hadn't been completely flipped upside down.

"Look," she said as the residential homes gave way to commercial buildings in Muellersville's small shopping district. "The ice cream parlor is open."

"Why wouldn't it be?" Cookie asked, not looking up from her phone.

"Everyone was panicking about the fires," Martina said. "It's nice to see them open. Should we get some ice cream?"

"Are you kidding?" Cookie asked.

"No." Martina looked perplexed. "Do people joke about wanting ice cream?"

"I think she's wondering if now is the right time to have ice cream," Farshad explained. Martina reminded him a little of some of his older Iranian relatives. Whenever they visited Muellersville, some things had to be explained, like why the town sometimes smelled like cows and how you shouldn't take photos of the Amish. Martina was like a visitor from a foreign land.

"Why not?" Martina asked. "Ice cream is delicious and might make us feel better."

Farshad's stomach was grumbling. He looked at Cookie. She was biting her lip.

"Okay. It's not like we can do anything at the hospital besides waiting," she said.

Ten minutes later, Farshad found himself sitting in an empty ice cream parlor with one girl who up until a little while ago he had considered to be his sworn enemy, and another whose eyes kept changing color. Martina was eating a mint chocolate chip cone, Farshad had a swirl of soft-serve chocolate and vanilla, and Cookie opted for a small cup of pistachio ice cream.

"Really?" Farshad had asked when she made her order.

"What?" Cookie snapped. "Was I supposed to get cookies 'n' cream?"

"Well . . ." Farshad didn't actually know what he'd expected her to get.

"I can like different things."

"Okay."

"I'm multifaceted."

"This is nice," Martina said, sighing happily. "I've never had ice cream with friends before."

Farshad and Cookie exchanged a look, which was interrupted by the sound of the ice cream parlor door opening. Cookie stopped eating. "Farts," she whispered.

Farshad looked up to see Emma Lee and her family coming into the shop. Emma's little brother was dragging her toward the counter. "Come on, come on!" he demanded. Emma walked right past them. Cookie put her hand over her eyes as if she were avoiding looking into the sun.

"Hey, I know her," Martina said. "She goes to our school and laughs at people when they get hurt."

Farshad looked at Cookie. She must have known that hiding her eyes wasn't going to camouflage her. If Emma looked at them, she was bound to see the only black girl in all of Muellersville sitting with the only Terror Boy in all of Muellersville. He almost felt sorry for her.

The Lee family ordered their ice creams to go and were heading back out the door when Emma glanced over at their table. Her mouth dropped open. "Cookie?" she asked.

"Come ON," Emma's little brother growled as he dragged her out of the parlor. "It's going to be all melty by the time we get home if you don't come on already!" And they were gone.

"Terrific," Cookie said. "Just great." She looked like she was about to start crying.

"What's wrong?" Martina asked.

Cookie shook her head.

"She's just upset because Emma Lee saw her eating with us," Farshad explained.

"Oh." Martina thought about it for a moment. "Is it because you're eating pistachio ice cream and that's weird?"

"No, it's because Emma Lee is going to tell everyone that the great and mighty Cookie Parker is now a big old loser who hangs out with other big old losers," Farshad said, shooting a hard look at Cookie. She looked up at him as if she were about to argue, but then fell silent and looked back down at her ice cream.

"Oh," Martina said. "I think my feelings might be hurt."

Cookie pushed her ice cream away. "You're not a loser," she said weakly. "Emma Lee is the biggest blabbermouth in school," she went on, "and I just don't need her spreading rumors about me."

"Like you spread rumors about, oh, everyone?" Farshad snapped.

Cookie thought for a moment. "Yeah," she said.

Farshad felt depleted. It was unsettling to hear her agree with him after he'd ripped into her. She looked troubled, and everyone at the table was silent for a minute.

"I'm sorry," she said finally, looking at Farshad. "I'm really sorry."

Of all the things that Farshad had ever imagined would come out of Cookie Parker's mouth, an apology was not one of them. He felt embarrassed. "It's okay," he mumbled.

"It's not and you know it," she said. "I'm sorry for all the things I said about you."

"What did you say about him?" Martina asked.

Farshad took a deep breath. "She's been telling everyone that I'm a terrorist."

Martina started to laugh. Cookie and Farshad stared at her, and she laughed harder, until she was clutching her sides. "Really?" She kept laughing. "And people believed you? That's ridiculous! Who would believe that?"

"Pretty much everyone," Cookie admitted, which sent Martina into another laughing fit.

"Wait, wait," she said, trying to catch her breath. "So you managed to convince pretty much everyone that a twelve-year-old is a terrorist, and you're worried about what Emma Lee will say about *you*? You could just tell everyone that *she's* a terrorist. Or a vampire! Or a unicorn! Or you could convince pretty much everyone that Farshad is a secret government double agent! Or a space alien." Martina's eyes turned a silvery gray. "You really don't know your own power."

"I like that," Farshad said. "Tell everyone I'm a space alien."

Cookie scowled. "That's stupid."

"Go on," Martina said. "Tell me that Farshad is a space alien."

"No."

"Go ahead," Farshad said.

Cookie took a deep breath. "Fine. Farshad is a space alien."

"I believe you!" Martina exclaimed, and Farshad found himself laughing with her. Cookie stared at them for a moment before giving in and joining the laughter. "Today has been so weird," she said when they'd all calmed down.

"Like your love of pistachio ice cream," Martina said, giggling a little to herself. Farshad laughed. Cookie put her hand to her temple and stopped eating.

Farshad recognized that look. "Is it Mr. Friend?"

"No," Cookie said, standing up. "But someone is trying to find Nick at the hospital."

"Let's go," Farshad said.

NICK SAT IN THE CHAIR NEXT TO HIS MOTHER'S HOSpital bed and watched her sleep. It was an all-too-familiar scene for him, only this time there were far fewer beeping machines and tubes and wires. He had to remind himself that she wasn't sick, that she was just resting. She was going to be fine.

They'd been told that the damage to Nick's house was superficial, and someone from the insurance agency was going to stop by in the morning to assess the damages. Nick really didn't like the idea of someone poking around his house and assigning monetary value to all of his things. What if their photo albums had been incinerated? How much money were they going to be awarded for losing photos of his young and healthy parents holding him as a baby?

His mother had inhaled a lot of smoke, and the doctors at Muellersville Memorial wanted to keep her overnight for observation. Two hospital stays in two nights for the Gross family—it was like old times; a bad joke that Nick hated thinking about and wouldn't dare tell his mother. He leaned forward, put his hand on hers for a moment, and stood up to leave.

Jay was waiting for Nick outside his mother's room with a cup of hospital cafeteria coffee in his hand. Nick let himself smile a little. Jay had finally gotten his caffeine fix.

"How's Angela?" Jay asked. His eyes were still a little puffy from crying.

"Sleeping," Nick said, sinking down into the seat next to Jay.

"My dad is on his way," Jay said. "The nurses let me call him and he's picking us up and you're staying over." That made sense. Nick and Jay spent most weekend nights at each other's houses anyway. He probably still had clothing there. Nick looked forward to changing and not smelling like the inside of a smokestack. "Also," Jay said with a waggle of his eyebrows, "I think I saw Ms. Zelle walking down the hall. She was probably here to comfort you."

"Sure she was," Nick said, acting nonchalant but peeking down the hallway all the same. But instead of Ms. Zelle, he saw Cookie, Farshad, and Martina making their way toward them.

Martina reached him first. "You smell like smoke," she observed.

"Did you just sniff me?"

Cookie stepped forward. "Someone is trying to find you."

Nick froze. "Mr. Friend?"

"No," she said, wrinkling her nose. "Someone else." She turned and looked down the hall, where a teenager dressed in black pants and a plain white shirt stood. He was holding a straw hat.

"Him," Cookie said.

IT WAS A STRANGE SCENE. COOKIE, FARSHAD, NICK, MAR-
tina, Jay, and the teenager who introduced himself to them
as Abe Zook sat around a table in the hospital cafeteria.
Abe looked extremely uncomfortable. Jay had another cup
of coffee.

"What did you do to Mr. Friend?" Nick asked Abe.

"He is safe," Abe said, looking down at his hands. "I think."

"Uh, you think?" Cookie asked. "You jumped off the back of
a horse and tackled him to the ground."

"I feel very bad about that."

"Sure," Cookie said. "Aren't you Amish supposed to, you know, not hurt anybody?"

"Now, now, Daniesha," Jay said quickly, "we cannot claim to understand the intricacies of a culture which we are but mere casual observers. Let's not fall prey to the vagaries of assumptions!"

Farshad shook his head. "Look, I don't know what you think you're doing, but Mr. Friend is a pretty dangerous guy. Wherever you have him, you've got to turn him in to the authorities."

"But he tells me not to." Abe looked tortured.

"Mr. Friend?" Cookie asked.

Abe looked around and lowered his voice. "No. The ghost."

Nick looked at Cookie, who looked at Farshad, who looked at Martina, who was sketching something in her book, so he looked back at Abe instead. "Ghost?" Nick asked.

"Fantastic," Jay breathed.

"What are you talking about?" Cookie asked.

Abe lowered his voice. "Since the night of the accident, a ghost has been speaking to me. He sent me to get the Fire Man and he sent me back to talk to you."

"So, did you hit your head in the crash?" Farshad asked. "Because some of us hit our heads. Hitting your head might make you feel a little . . ."

"Completely nuts?" Cookie offered.

"I wasn't in the accident," the teenager said, frowning. "Your bus almost ran me over but swerved out of the way. Then, after everyone was out, I went to get help, and that's when the ghost started talking to me."

"Extraordinary!" Jay said, leaping up from his seat. "Our man Abe here has the ABILITY TO SPEAK TO THE DEAD."

"Sit down!" Farshad hissed at the same time as Cookie growled, "Shut it!"

"I am sorry, my dearest, but I will not shut it. This is amazing. Do you know what this means? It means that we can communicate with those who are no longer with us!"

"No," Nick said, "no, we can't. There are no such things as ghosts." He gave his friend a hard look, and Jay looked down and fell silent. "There is another explanation for what's going on." He looked at Abe. "What did the ghost want you to tell us?"

"He wanted me to let you know not to worry about the Fire Man anymore. He wanted you to know that you are now safe from him."

"Goody," Cookie said, "I feel totally reassured."

Farshad looked perplexed. "So where's Mr. Friend?"

"He's at my farm," Abe said. "The ghost says that he can take care of him there and keep him safe until . . ."

"Until what?" Nick asked.

"Until the ghost and his friend can figure out what's wrong with him."

"So your ghost has a friend?" asked Farshad.

"Is it another ghost?" asked Jay.

"There is no ghost," Cookie said. She stood up. "Someone is messing with you. Someone is messing with all of us, and that someone knows what happened to us during that accident. Let's go." She looked each of them in the eye and felt like her old, unstoppable self.

"I'm with Daniesha," Jay said with fervor.

"No," Nick said. He looked down the hall to the room where his mother slept. Leaving her seemed crazy, but Cookie was right. He needed to know what had happened to him. She'd never know that he was gone. "Jay, I need you to stay here and tell your dad that my aunt picked me up." His best friend looked crestfallen. "I need you," Nick repeated.

"Of course," Jay said. "I understand that my role to play in this endeavor will be to hold the fort down. I will bear false witness to my own father so that you can make progress with your investigation. I will not fail you." He gave the group a quick, regretful look. "All I ask is that you think fondly of my sacrifice and you debrief me upon your return. Godspeed." Jay took a quick bow and then left the cafeteria.

"Whoever has Mr. Friend had better have answers for us," Cookie said as they walked out of the hospital.

"Or what?" Farshad asked.

"Or we'll *get* answers," Cookie said. She spun around and

looked at Abe, who immediately looked down at the ground. "You're taking us to your farm. Where is your car?"

"Hey, look, a horse," Martina said, pointing at a horse and buggy that was parked in the visitors' lot of the hospital.

"You're kidding me," Nick said.

"I know that horse," Farshad said.

Cookie marched up grimly to the buggy, took a deep breath, and climbed inside. Martina and Nick followed, and Farshad climbed onto the front bench next to Abe.

"Take us to your ghost," he said.

COOKIE HAD NEVER BEEN IN A HORSE-DRAWN buggy before. She had seen them plenty of times, trotting down the county roads around Muellersville and gumming up traffic, as well as in the historical areas of Philadelphia, where tourists paid to be shown the sights from high up in a fancy open carriage. When she was little, she'd always wanted to go on a ride, but would never in a million years have guessed this was how she'd end up in one.

The buggy was much, much faster than she would have predicted—once they hit the road out of town it seemed like they were going as fast as a car.

"Did we just pass that truck?" Nick asked. The whole buggy was shaking and it was hard to hear him over the rattling of the wooden wheels flying down the pavement.

Martina looked out the small square window. "We just passed a bunch of cars," she shouted.

There were no seat belts. Of course. Cookie gripped her seat. "Is that normal?" she bleated. "I feel like that's not normal!"

"Maybe the cars are going really slow!" Martina yelled. Outside, the farmland flew by in the moonlight. They heard Farshad and Abe shouting something to each other, but couldn't figure out what. Nick looked green.

"Are you okay?" Cookie asked him. The buggy lurched, and

Nick, Cookie, and Martina were all thrown from their benches. They landed on the floor of the carriage in a jumbled heap.

"This is awkward!" Martina shouted.

"MMMRRPPHHH!" Nick tried to push Cookie off his face. She struggled to get up but was thrown backward into Martina as the buggy rocked back and forth.

"Gah! Hi!" Martina yelped.

"HOW FAST ARE WE GOING?" Cookie yelled to Farshad.

"VERY!" they heard Farshad yelling back.

"ARE WE GOING TO DIE?" Nick hollered.

"POSSIBLY!"

"CAN YOU TELL ABE TO SLOW THE HELL DOWN?" Cookie screamed.

"HE SAYS THE HORSE DOESN'T WANT TO SLOW DOWN!" Farshad sounded terrified.

"I TRULY DO NOT CARE WHAT THE HORSE WANTS!"

"Do you think the horse has super speed?" Martina wondered aloud.

"Oh my god." Cookie stared at her before tumbling on top of Nick again.

"WE'RE GOING TO DIE," Nick said.

NICK HADN'T EATEN ANYTHING SINCE HE'D THROWN up in his yard after the fire, and he was glad for it because there was nothing left for his stomach to expel. Once they were off the country road, the buggy slowed down and the horse ambled at a reasonable speed until they stopped in front of a large barn. Nick tumbled out of the cab and immediately fell to the ground, as if he'd just disembarked from a boat that had been through a tidal wave. The others didn't look so hot but managed to remain upright. Abe helped Nick up off the ground.

"I don't like your horse," Nick told him.

"The ghost has her really spooked," Abe said. "I've never seen her run as fast as she has since he showed up."

"Have you ever seen *any* horse run that fast?" Cookie asked.

"No, but we don't have call for a lot of fancy racing horses on the farm," Abe said.

"Well, let's see what we can do about this ghost situation," Cookie said. "Where is he?"

"Probably with the Fire Man," Abe said, pointing to the barn.

"In the highly flammable wooden barn?" Farshad asked as Abe pushed open the large barn doors.

The inside of the barn smelled like animal farts. There were sleeping cows and pigs and, from what Nick could hear, more than a few chickens. In the center of the barn, lit by lantern light, lay Mr. Friend on a cot under a quilt.

"Is he dead?" Cookie asked.

"No, he is sleeping." Abe looked around nervously. "The ghost gave him something to help him sleep," he whispered.

"Shady," Cookie muttered.

"Is the . . . ghost here right now?" Farshad asked, looking around the barn.

"Yes," Martina said, pointing to the empty chair next to the cot. "He's sitting right there." She waved at the chair.

"You can see me?" a voice asked. It was a man's voice, and it sounded familiar.

"Sure," Martina said. "Can't everyone?"

"No," Cookie, Nick, Farshad, and the voice said at the same time. Abe looked shocked.

"Oh," Martina said. "Well, he's right over there. It's the bus driver."

For a moment no one spoke. "Oh thank god," the bus driver said finally. "I'm so glad you can see me. No one has been able to see me since the accident."

Mr. Friend let out a small moan and everyone took a step back.

"Don't worry," the bus driver said, "he's not going to hurt anyone."

"Were you able to take away his . . . power?" Cookie asked, looking desperately at the chair.

"He's standing next to me now." Martina pointed.

"Whatever," Cookie said dismissively. "Can Mr. Friend still explode stuff?"

"I don't know," the bus driver said. "But probably. I needed to calm him down so he couldn't hurt anyone. I gave him some horse tranquilizer."

"So, you aren't a ghost?" Abe asked, looking around the inside of the barn in a fruitless attempt to see the bus driver.

"No, Abe, I told you, my name is Ed," the bus driver said. "I'm afraid I've completely confused him." He sighed.

"He's not the only one that's confused. What happened to us?" Cookie asked.

"What happened to you?" Ed asked. "Tell me exactly what happened to you."

"Everything has been . . . different since the accident," Farshad said with a warning in his voice. Nick understood. Cookie caught his eye. She got it. *Don't give the Invisible Man any details.*

"Nick can teleport and Farshad can crush things and Cookie can read minds and my eyes keep changing color," Martina said. "Oh, and I can see invisible people. And I think that Abe's horse has super speed."

"Martina!" Cookie growled.

"What?"

"The horse has super speed?" Ed asked. Cookie still had no idea where to look.

"That would explain a great deal," Abe murmured to himself.

"Ed," Cookie said, taking a step toward Martina but looking at the area nearish to her. "Tell us what's going on. You brought Mr. Friend here, so clearly you think that you can help him. And if you can help him, that means you know what's wrong with him."

"And what's wrong with us," said Nick.

"And you can fix us," Cookie said.

The empty space next to Martina let out a deep sigh. "I don't know exactly what to tell you."

"Start with everything," Cookie said angrily. "Because the bus crash was your fault. We got hurt because of you. You owe us."

"I never meant to hurt any of you." Ed said, and they heard the sound of his feet shuffling the hay on the floor as he moved across the barn. "I was doing a favor for my brother. He knew I was driving to Philadelphia and needed me to deliver something to one of his colleagues."

"What were you delivering?" Cookie asked.

"Who's your brother?" Farshad asked.

"So you really aren't a ghost?" Abe asked. "Are you sure? Maybe you died in the crash."

"Abe," Nick said, "there was no dead body. He's invisible.

The crash did something weird to us and made him invisible and your horse completely insane."

Mr. Friend moaned in his sleep.

"Wait," Cookie said. "Someone is coming." She looked frightened. "Someone is looking for Mr. Friend."

"How do you know that?" Ed asked.

"She knows," Farshad said.

"How far away are they?"

"We should hide," Cookie said, her voice urgent. She headed to the back of the barn. Farshad grabbed Martina, and Nick watched as the invisible bus driver lifted up a groaning Mr. Friend. It looked like Yo-Yo Sub was floating, ungracefully, in midair. The bus driver must have had him over his shoulder.

"Here, here," Abe said, herding the kids up a ladder to a hayloft. "Get under the hay," he whispered.

"Ew, no," Cookie said as Martina dragged her underneath a pile. Outside, they heard the sound of a car engine. "Who is it?" Nick whispered to Cookie, who was peeking out from underneath the hay to watch the moaning body of Mr. Friend float into one of the empty animal stalls below them.

"I don't know but she sounded really . . . cold."

"She?"

"Shhh." Farshad clapped his hand over Nick's mouth and pointed to the open door of the barn.

It was Ms. Zelle.

FARSHAD HELD HIS BREATH. HE KNEW THAT HE SHOULD have felt relieved to see Ms. Zelle. She was an adult, and the science club adviser, and she could give them all a lift back to town in a vehicle that probably wasn't going to kill them. But he stayed quiet. He was good at that.

Farshad could make out the details of Ms. Zelle's face in the lantern light. "Ryan?" she called out again. "I know you're in here. It's okay. You can come out." She began walking through the barn, peeking her head over the stalls. Her high heels made her wobble on the uneven dirt floor.

"Excuse me." Abe stepped out from underneath the hayloft. "You are in my family's barn."

"Where is Ryan?" Ms. Zelle asked. "I know you brought him here."

"This is not your barn. You should go," Abe said.

"And you should tell me where Ryan is," Ms. Zelle said, reaching into her bag and pulling out a Taser. She pointed it at Abe. The electricity from the tip of the gun crackled, illuminating her face. She looked terrifying.

"Whut," Farshad heard Cookie say next to him.

"WHERE. IS. HE," Ms. Zelle demanded, her face contorting. Abe took a step back. In the stall, Mr. Friend let out a groan.

"Ryan?" Ms. Zelle asked. "Ryan, it's Maggie. Can you hear my voice?"

"Maggie . . . ?" Mr. Friend's voice was slurred but he definitely didn't sound asleep.

"This is not good," Nick whispered.

"You think?" Cookie hissed.

Martina pointed to Ms. Zelle. A moment later the Taser flew out of her hand and her body began to contort.

"Are you doing that?" Nick gasped, looking at Martina.

"No, the bus driver is. He's trying to keep her from getting the electricity gun."

"Ohhh. Right."

Ms. Zelle might not have been able to see who she was fighting, but she was definitely fighting back. Gone was the wobble in her step: She was fighting like someone who had been trained in martial arts. It was one of the most disturbing and coolest things Farshad had ever seen. "Whoa," Cookie said next to him, lifting her head farther out of the haystack. They could hear the bus driver panting with exertion. He may have been invisible, but he clearly wasn't some sort of ninja warrior.

"Ooof!" Abe fell to the ground below them and Farshad watched in frozen horror as Mr. Friend emerged from behind him, holding a shovel in his hands.

"Maggie?" he asked, lurching unsteadily toward the flailing science teacher.

"Ryan, help me!" Ms. Zelle yelled, and Mr. Friend took a swing with the shovel. It landed midair with a dull thud, fol-

lowed by a second thud as Ed the bus driver's body hit the ground. Farshad looked at Martina.

"He hit him in the butt," Martina whispered. "He's down but I don't think he's dead."

"Maggie . . . ," Mr. Friend said as Ms. Zelle scrambled to pick up the Taser. "Maggie, what's going on? Where am I? I was trying to find you . . ."

She walked across the barn and hugged him. "It's okay. It's going to be okay."

"Maggie," Mr. Friend said, "there are people. Bad people. They tried to take me out of the hospital, but I didn't want to go . . . We have to get away from them . . ."

"Don't worry," Ms. Zelle said. "You're going to be all right. I'm going to take you back to the hospital."

Mr. Friend took a step back. "We can't go back there," he said, his voice shaking. "You have to listen to me. They came to my room and tried to make me come with them. We can't go back!" He began to hyperventilate.

"Ryan," Ed's voice called out weakly, "you have to stay calm."

Ms. Zelle's head swiveled back and forth, trying to ascertain where the sound was coming from.

"There's another car coming," Cookie whispered.

"Come on, Ryan," Ms. Zelle said. "Come with me. I know people who can help you. Just come with me."

"Don't trust her," Ed pleaded. "She's one of *them*."

Mr. Friend looked around frantically and a pile of hay behind Ms. Zelle burst into flames. Cookie gasped. Farshad felt his heart racing. They had to get out. He was not going to die in a fiery barn in the middle of Amish country.

"Come on!" Ms. Zelle yelled. "Let's get out of here. Come with me!"

Mr. Friend stumbled to where Abe was lying on the ground. "Help me!" he yelled, trying to lift him up.

"Leave him!" Ms. Zelle screamed as the flames climbed up the frame of the barn. "We have to get out of here!"

"We can't let him burn!" Mr. Friend pleaded.

"We most certainly can." Ms. Zelle lifted her gun and shot Mr. Friend. He screamed and convulsed before passing out. Two men in hazmat jackets burst into the barn. "Took you long enough," Ms. Zelle snapped as they hauled Mr. Friend out of the building. "When you've got him situated, there's another one in here somewhere. Invisibility . . ."

A huge flaming crossbeam fell from the ceiling, and Ms. Zelle ran out of the building. The fire was spreading.

"What do we do?" Cookie screamed.

Farshad looked around. "Where's Ed?" he asked Martina.

"He's trying to get Abe," she said. Below, they could hear the awful sounds of terrified animals squealing and stomping in their stalls.

Farshad stood up and ran to the back wall of the hayloft.

He pressed his hands to the wall, trying not to inhale the rising smoke, and pushed at the wood with his thumbs. A large section of wall burst out and fell two stories to the ground. Cookie ran up to Farshad and grabbed his arm before he could plummet down after the shattered planks of wood.

"We'll break every bone in our bodies if we jump!" she yelled.

"Probably not every bone," Martina said, "but we will be in some pain." She began grabbing bales of hay and hurling them out of the hole in the wall. Farshad, Nick, and Cookie joined her, and soon there was a decent-size pile.

Cookie looked at Farshad. "This sucks," she said, taking a few steps back and then running to hurl herself out of the hole. Farshad, Nick, and Martina looked down to see her lying in the pile of hay.

"That sucked!" she yelled, scrambling off the pile to make room for the others.

Martina went next, clutching her backpack and yelling, "WHEEEEEE!" all the way down.

Farshad looked at Nick. "Let's do this."

"I do not like being a superhero!" Nick yelled as they plummeted down to the haystack.

"We have to get Abe and the animals!" Martina gasped once they were all on solid ground. "We have to find a way to get them out!"

Everyone looked at Farshad.

"Didn't I just get everyone out of the fiery barn?" he asked. "What, now you want to go back in?"

Martina gave him two thumbs up. Farshad rolled his eyes and headed to the back of the barn, using his thumbs to blast another hole in the wall. It was smaller than the first, but large enough for Nick, Cookie, and Martina to reach in and pull away pieces until they could all see what was inside.

The animals were gathered together in the center of the barn, which had become a blazing inferno. But no flames touched them, or Abe, who was standing in the middle of the sheep and the goats and the horses.

"Cool," Martina whispered.

"Abe!" Nick shouted. "Abe, buddy! We're over here! Come here!" Abe's eyes opened and he slowly began walking through the fire toward them. The animals calmly moved with him without seeming the slightest bit affected by the flames or the smoke.

"Wow," Martina breathed.

"Is Ed with him?" Cookie asked her.

"No," Martina said. "But I'm pretty sure he made it out."

Nick looked worried. "Are you sure, or pretty sure?"

Martina looked off into the fields behind the burning barn. Her eyes were bright blue. "He's okay."

The group backed away as Abe and the animals emerged

from the back of the barn to safety. In the distance Farshad could see people running toward the blaze. Abe watched the animals he saved ambling farther away from the barn to safety.

"We have to get out of here," Cookie said. "I am never going to be able to explain this to my mom."

"I can give you a ride back into town," Abe said, glancing across the darkened fields at the people headed their way. "There are some questions I really don't know how to answer right now, either."

"Is there maybe a different horse you could use?" Nick asked.

THE DAILY WHUT?

It has been four days since the fire at the Zook farm, and the alleged Muellersville arsonist, Ryan Friend, is still on the loose. Should we be frightened? YES. WE SHOULD BE TERRIFIED FOR OUR LIVES.

There are those among us who just want to cheer and say, "Oh The Hammer, why do you have to be so negative? It's all over. There were some fires, but no one got hurt, so everything is just A-OK." I'll tell you why I'm so negative. It's because NONE OF THIS MAKES SENSE.

Do you know where Ryan Friend was on Thursday evening? He was still in the hospital recuperating from the school bus accident. What sort of person goes to work teaching kids, is in an accident that puts him in the hospital, and then while he is still in the hospital decides to start setting cars on fire? I don't know about you, inquisitive reader, but last month I had a slight head cold and I didn't want to leave the house, let alone run around setting fire to things. Now, as some commenters have pointed out, yes, Ryan Friend was just a substitute teacher, so we don't know a whole lot about him, but isn't that in and of itself something to question? Who is Ryan Friend? How did he

THE DAILY WHUT?

get hired? Did Principal Jacobs hire him? Was there any sort of background check? Is he a deranged firebug, or just an unattached and therefore convenient scapegoat? And why did he end up in the middle of Amish country?

Something about this whole situation stinks, and it's a smell stronger than burning cow poop. But don't worry, dear reader: The Hammer is on the case.

Keep asking questions,
The Hammer

ACKNOWLEDGMENTS

I would like to thank all of the amazing people at Abrams Books who have worked so tirelessly to bring this book to the world: Maggie Lehrman, Chad Beckerman, Jason Wells, Caitlin Miller, Maria Middleton, Michael Clark, and of course my wonderful editor, Susan Van Metre, who never hesitates to follow me into the deep end of the pool of absurdity.

Thank you to Tori Doherty-Munro at Writers House, and to my beloved agent Dan Lazar, who for the past decade has been thoughtfully considering every wackadoo idea I feel the need to email him at four in the morning.

Much thanks as well to Leeann Wallett and the wonderful staff at the National Constitution Center for letting me run around their offices with a camera.

Thank you so much to all the friends and family members who have been so supportive and inspirational, as well as all of the librarians and booksellers and bloggers and readers. Special thanks to my children for being terrific nappers, and to Mark for always loving me, challenging me, believing in me, and shoveling all the snow.

AMY IGNATOW

is the author/illustrator of the acclaimed series The Popularity Papers. She is a graduate of Moore College of Art and Design and lives in Philadelphia with her husband and their children.

★ ★ ★ ★ ★

**A sneak peek at the
second book in
the ODDS series**

The Muelle

Local Muellersville Educator Wanted for Arson

The Muellersville Police Department is seeking the whereabouts of local substitute teacher Ryan Friend, 28, who is wanted for questioning in regard to a series of arsons. He was last witnessed fleeing the scene of a house fire on Tall Oaks Drive.

The homeowner, Angela Gross, was able to escape the blaze but suffered from smoke inhalation. "I have no idea why anyone would want to do this to us," the single mother said from her hospital bed. "But I hope they catch the guy before he can hurt anyone else."

"He seemed like a nice enough man," said Charlene Beckerman, who went on three dates with Mr. Friend two years ago but chose not to continue the relationship because "he took his yo-yo everywhere and that was kind of weird."

His students were less charitable. "One time he sent me to the assistant principal's office and I hardly did anything," said Izaak Marcus, an eighth grader at Deborah Read Middle School who often had Mr. Friend as a substitute teacher. "And you could tell that even though he was saying, 'Izaak, go see Mr. Deutsch,' what he really meant was, 'Izaak, I totally want to set you on fire!'"

Local police did not want to speculate about the motive behind Mr. Friend's alleged arsonist tendencies. "Look, we just want to ask the guy some questions," Chief Gary Romaine told *The Muellersville Sun*, "while maybe holding on to a fire extinguisher."

THE DAILY WHUT?

WHERE IS RYAN FRIEND?

That's right, faithful readers, The Hammer has made the artistic choice to press down on the CAPS LOCK button because I can't believe that a suspected arsonist is still running around Muellersville. Where will he strike next? Whose house or car will go up in flames? Why aren't the police more concerned? WHERE'S THE MANHUNT?

I'll tell you why there isn't a manhunt. It's because RYAN FRIEND IS INNOCENT. Isn't it just so convenient that the only suspect that the police have is a substitute teacher with no friends or family nearby. The only person that *The Muellersville Sun* could find to say anything about him was some lady who went on three dates with him two years ago. But longtime readers of *The Daily Whut* know very well that *The Muellersville Sun* is in the pocket of local law enforcement and possesses the journalistic integrity of a ham sandwich. A HAM SANDWICH WITH NO JOURNALISTIC INTEGRITY.

Oh, Hammer, you say, you're making crazy, unfounded statements again. Am I? AM I REALLY? Let's all remember the time that I was right about Freshtush toilet paper rolls getting shorter so that the company could make more money per roll. My track record is spotless, which is more than I can say for The Muellersville Ham Sandwich.

Ryan Friend never once showed any violent tendencies. He was a substitute teacher who loved yo-yos and occasionally sent a deserving little twerp to the principal's office. He wasn't some highly trained firebug with the ability to vanish into thin air.

WHERE IS RYAN FRIEND?

Ever questioning,
The Hammer

**KAY, LET'S GO OVER IT AGAIN." JAY WAS PACING** the length of his room, unable to contain his energy. Nick hadn't seen his best friend this worked up since The Hammer's blog had convinced him that there was methylphenidate in the Muellersville town water supply. That time Jay had worked himself into such a frenzy that he'd begun to hyperventilate. Nick's mom had made Jay breathe into a paper bag to calm down. Nick scanned Jay's room for a paper bag.

"I don't know what else to tell you," he said. It was too early in the morning for Jay's energy.

"Nick. Nick. NICK. Last night you saw AN INVISIBLE MAN," Jay yelled, throwing his hands up in the air. Nick thought about telling him to quiet down, but it wasn't as if Jay's parents weren't used to their son's nonsensical rants. They were probably tuning him out, as usual.

"Well, technically I didn't actually see anything," Nick pointed out.

"Amazing. AMAZING. And not true—you say that he picked up Mr. Friend, so you saw Mr. Friend LEVITATING. Now tell me that wasn't amazing!"

Nick had to grin. "Okay, that was pretty cool."

"Pretty cool?" Jay threw his hands up in the air. "Nick, old sport, your gift for understatement is magnificent. So let's review. You, Martina, Farshad, *and* the Amish lad, *and* the bus driver, *and* the ravishing Miss Daniesha Parker all have super-powers."

"Jay, you seriously have to stop calling Cookie 'ravishing.' I'm pretty sure she doesn't like it."

"Nonsense, all women love to be complimented. Especially ravishing ones with superpowers."

Nick sighed. "I wouldn't call them superpowers, exactly. They're not that super." Nick thought a moment. "Except the horse. I think Abe's horse had super speed."

"I . . . I can't even deal with that right now. But Amish Abe can *control animals and protect them from a flaming inferno*??? And the bus driver is INVISIBLE."

"Yeah, but he can't seem to get visible again. That's not so super."

"Wait." Jay froze. "Wait wait wait. Was the bus driver naked?"

"What? Ew! No. I don't think so. How would I know? I couldn't see him."

"Ugh, Nicholas, you are too squeamish about nudity. It's the body's natural state. If I had my druthers, I'd be naked all the time." Jay spread his spindly arms and gazed off into the distance, as if he were imagining a world where he could be un-encumbered by clothing. Then he looked perplexed. "Although I don't know what I'd do for pockets."

"Maybe a purse? Like, a manly one?" Nick asked. Sometimes he wondered how Jay roped him into these conversations, but it was usually pretty entertaining to go with the flow.

"That would give me a strange tan line."

"I don't recall ever seeing you tan."

"It would give me an odd burn line. So what you're saying, though, is that the bus driver could have been naked."

"I don't know." Nick thought a moment. "Martina would probably have told us if he was naked, right?" Martina was the only one who had been able to see the invisible bus driver. Maybe the power to change her eye color had something to do with her ability to see Ed?

"Hmmm. The alluring Miss Martina seems like the sort who would be good at keeping secrets about nudity." Jay flopped down on top of the bed, and then flopped around some more to get comfortable. He looked like a fish that had just been pulled out of the water and placed on a dry dock. "Let's say the driver isn't naked," Jay mused.

"Yes, let's say that," Nick agreed.

"If he isn't, that means that it is within his power to turn other things invisible." Jay jumped back to his feet. "Just like it's within your power to move things with you, like your clothing and small pebbles that you are holding, when you teleport!!!"

"Shhh!" Nick said, his eyes darting to Jay's bedroom door. Jay scoffed. "Please, it's as if you haven't been here a million times.

They're not listening in." He raised his voice. "AND THAT'S WHEN WE WILL ALL SUBMIT TO OUR ALIEN OVER-LORDS. WE WILL GIVE THEM ALL THE CORN CHOWDER AND THEY SHALL REWARD US WITH THE EURASIAN STEPPE." Jay fell silent and looked at Nick. "I could tell them to their faces about your power and they still wouldn't hear me."

He had a point. For as long as Nick had known Jay (forever), the Carpenters had never paid too much attention to him, as long as he got good grades and tested well. Still, Jay needed to get in the habit of being a little more discreet. If Cookie Parker heard him talking in public about their powers, she'd end the little weirdo.

Nick grabbed Jay's wrist and looked at the watch he always wore. "Molly is going to be here soon," he said. "She's probably already on her way." He didn't want to keep his aunt waiting and felt bad enough about leaving his mother alone in her hospital room the night before.

"How long are you staying with your aunts?" Jay asked. "You know you could just stay here until your house is ready. My parents wouldn't care."

"Thanks," Nick said, "but my mom is going to stay with them, and I want to be with her." The doctor at the hospital had assured Nick and his aunts that his mom was going to be fine, but he was still worried about her. She'd looked so fragile. Plus his aunts always made good food like spaghetti and meatballs, while the Carpenters had once pressured Nick into eating raw sea urchin. Avoiding that was alone worth sleeping on the nursery futon at Molly and Jilly's house.

"I understand, old boy," Jay said, "but you have to promise to tell me the minute there are any developments on your ... odd situation."

Nick promised and headed out to wait on the curb for his aunt. As soon as he sat down, he felt the four-inch shift to the left as he inadvertently teleported.

"Oh, come on," he muttered under his breath, gripping the curb with both of his hands in a desperate attempt to stay put before teleporting four inches to the left again. "You have got to be kidding me."

FARSHAD RAJAVI STARED IN DISMAY AT THE RUINS OF what just one minute before had been his father's functioning laptop. The space bar was crushed, and the practice test on the screen flickered and blurred. Farshad stared for a moment at his hands before closing his eyes.

I'll just tell him I dropped something on it, he decided, and grimaced at the thought of lying to either of his parents. Lying was something that Farshad had never done before the bus accident had turned him into a great big freak. Sure, there had been plenty of times when he hadn't been completely honest, but flat-out lying was new.

He opened his eyes and looked around the room for something that would be heavy enough to cause the damage that his abnormally strong thumbs had caused. There were a few heavy-looking books, a framed photo of Farshad with his family in front of the Azadi Tower in Tehran, and a trophy from when he used to play soccer. He picked up the trophy. Plastic. Too light. The books weren't going to cut it either. He was going to have to take the framed photograph and let it drop to the floor. *The glass will probably smash*, Farshad thought, *and then maybe they'll be so upset that the photo is messed up that they won't even think too hard about the laptop.*

Farshad took the frame off the wall and looked at the smiling faces in the photo, which had been taken while they were visiting family a few years ago. He placed the frame back on the hook on the wall, taking care not to put too much pressure on it with his thumbs. What had he been thinking? And why had he never considered taking up bowling as a sport? Having a bowling ball would have been really useful right about now. Farshad sighed, shut the laptop, and headed downstairs. He'd just use the computer lab at school to finish the test and figure out what to do about the laptop later.

"You're up early." His mother looked at him worriedly as he grabbed his jacket. "What is up?"

"I'm just going to school a little early," Farshad told her. "There's a pre-homeroom study group meetup." *Lying lies told by a lying liar.*

"Ah, yes," Dr. Rajavi nodded. "The exam is coming up. Are you ready?"

"I will be," he said, grabbing a croissant from the bag on top of the fridge and shoving it into his mouth. If there was one thing his parents would never stop him from doing, it was studying. He gave his mom a quick kiss on the cheek and headed out the front door.

Farshad kept his head down as he walked to school, just like he'd done since the fourth grade, when he'd become the class pariah because his parents were Persian (or "terrorists" as his idiot classmates liked to whisper behind his back . . . and say out loud in front of his face). Stooping down made Farshad appear to be shorter than he was so that people would notice him less, which, when he thought about it, was another type of lying. But lying to protect yourself seemed a lot better than telling the truth and getting hurt. Look at Mr. Friend. If he had just been able to control his power and then lie about being able to set things on fire with his mind, he wouldn't be . . .

Where was he? Where had they taken Mr. Friend? And who were *they*?

The ride home from the farm had been pretty quiet. Nick Gross had been worried about his mom, Cookie Parker had been cursing under her breath as she picked bits of straw out of her curls, and Martina Saltis had never been much of a talker in the first place. She had just looked out the window as the farmland turned into the suburbs, her eyes changing from blue to green to brown to a very disconcerting shade of violet. Farshad had a thousand questions and not much faith that any of his newfound Comrades in Lame Powers would be able to answer them, so he stayed quiet as well.

Abe had dropped them off near the school so they could all walk home. At the time, Farshad had been relieved to get out of the buggy (that horse was *fast*) and glad to have the short walk home to think about everything that had happened before he sneaked back into his house. When he got there, his parents hadn't even realized that he was missing. They had just assumed he'd been in his room, studying. It made sense;

besides running, studying in his room was all Farshad did, really. He thought about Cookie Parker and how she was always surrounded by a crowd of friends. She probably hadn't been able to sneak back home so easily.

Good, Farshad thought. They'd been through too much together for him to hate her like he used to, but the thought of Cookie getting into trouble still made him smile.

Farshad passed by a janitor and some teachers prepping lessons in their rooms. He was eager to finish the practice test; he might not be able to control the unbelievable strength in his thumbs, but he could do well on the exam, and right now it felt good to be in control of something in his life.

"No, Officer, I haven't seen Ryan since the accident." Farshad heard Mrs. Whitaker's voice. He stopped walking. "I just assumed he was recuperating. You don't really believe that he had anything to do with those fires, do you?"

Farshad pretended to open a locker near Mrs. Whitaker's classroom door and peeked in. She was talking with a uniformed police officer.

"We're just gathering information, ma'am." The officer said. "Had Mr. Friend been acting strangely before the accident?"

"No! I don't think so. I didn't know him that well. He was just a substitute."

"I understand. Did he ever mention any friends? Hobbies? Places he liked to go to when he wasn't at work?"

"Tahiti? Ha-ha, no, kidding, that's where I would like to go when I'm not at work."

"I hear that, ha-ha. Well, if you can think of anywhere he'd be or any person he'd spend time with . . ."

"Actually" — Mrs. Whitaker thought a moment — "I think he might have been seeing Maggie Zelle. You know. Romantically. Although I doubt it was anything serious."

"We've already spoken to Ms. Zelle," the officer said, "and she knows about as much as we do."

"Oh no, she knows way more — she's a science teacher, ha-ha-ha!"

"Ha-ha! Well, here's my card, let me know."

"Will do, Officer," Mrs. Whitaker said. Farshad heard the policeman heading toward the door and stared intently at the combination lock in front of him. The officer gave him a suspicious glance before heading down the hall. Farshad walked quickly to the computer lab. He logged into the practice test site and tried and failed to concentrate. He looked at his thumbs.

Where was Mr. Friend? And what was happening to him?